# Just So Stories

*Curated by Nicole Petit*

JUST SO STORIES
An 18thWall Productions book published by
arrangement with Nicole Petit
verba mea in minibus
desiderium meum
Cover and design by Elisgraphics
Text Copyright
Just So Stories © Nicole Petit
How the Firefly Found her Flame © Jan Snook
How Time Learned to be Bedtime © Pauline J. Alama
Mind Your P's and Q's © Robert Walden
The Nidibalan © Patricia S. Bowne
The Fruit Tree © Arthur Powers
Gravity's Final Hug © Russ Bickerstaff
How Duck Lost Her Voice © Ken MacGregor
How the Elephant Fell © Liam Hogan
Why the Sea is Salt © Edward Ahern

# Table of Contents

# Introduction
*Rudyard Kipling*

Some stories are meant to be read quietly and some stories are meant to be told aloud. Some stories are only proper for rainy mornings, and some for long, hot afternoons when one is lying in the open, and some stories are bedtime stories.

All the Blue Skalallatoot stories are morning tales (I do not know why, but that is what Effie says). All the stories about Orvin Sylvester Woodsey, the left-over New England fairy who did not think it well-seen to fly, and who used patent labour-saving devices instead of charms, are afternoon stories because they were generally told in the shade of the woods.

You could alter and change these tales as much as you pleased; but in the evening there were stories meant to put Effie to sleep, and you were not allowed to alter those by one single little word. They had to be told just so; or Effie would take up and put back the missing sentence. So at last they can be like charms, all three of them—the whale tale, the camel tale, and the rhinoceros tale.

Of course, little people are not alike, but I think if you catch some Effie rather tired and rather sleepy at the end of the day, and if you begin in a low voice an tell the tales precisely as I have written them down, you will find that Effie will presently curl up and go to sleep.

Now, this is the first tale. . .

# How the Firefly Found her Flame

*Jan Snook*

In the land of the Malays, once upon a time, O my Best Beloved, there lived a small brown beetle who dreamed of being beautiful. She lived in the jungle on the banks of the river, and was surrounded all day long by beautiful birds and butterflies, their colours flashing in the sunshine, or gleaming in the tropical rains.

"But I am just brown," said the little beetle. "Brown with beige stripes. And as ugly as sin."

"We agree," said the birds, the butterflies, and the shimmering dragonflies. "You are too ugly to be seen. Go. Away." And they called the small brown beetle *Pelik*, which means 'strange,' or 'odd,' in Malay. And soon everyone in the jungle called the beetle Pelik, even her own mother.

"Take no notice," Pelik's mother said serenely. "They may be beautiful on the outside—in a rather showy and obvious way—but you are full of beautiful and pure thoughts, and that is more important."

And this was true, O Best Beloved. No matter what unkind words were used of Pelik, she never said—or even thought—an unkind word herself.

However, the little beetle was not satisfied with her mother's answer.

"But no-one else can see my thoughts," she said. "To them I am just an ugly brown beetle called Pelik." (She pronounced it the Malay way, so that it sounded like Pleek, the sound of someone flicking a nasty bug out of their way.)

One day Pelik saw a beautiful dragonfly sunning itself on a large glossy leaf.

She gazed at it in wonder. "Oh Sibur-sibur," she said (for that is the word for 'dragonfly' in Malay), "how your wings sparkle and gleam so green, they shine, so elegant, delicate, gossamer-fine!"

"That's true," said the dragonfly, gazing at her beautiful wings, and then looking down at Pelik in disdain. "And you are so dark and dirty, shadowy, murky, you do nothing but spoil my view. You are too ugly to come out in the sun, go hide in a dark place until it is night. Then no-one will see you, you horrible sight!"

If anyone said that to me, Dearly Beloved, I should lecture them on manners, and stand my ground, but as you know, Pelik was different. No matter what unkind words were used of Pelik, she never said—or even thought—an unkind word herself.

So she wandered off, wondering where she

could spend her days so as not to offend any beautiful creatures. She hadn't gone very far when she felt a cool breeze on her back. She flew up and landed on the petal of a hibiscus flower, but was nearly blown off it by the gently waving wings of an enormous butterfly.

She gazed at it in wonder. "Oh Kupu-kupu," she said (for that is the word for 'butterfly' in Malay), "how wondrous, how gorgeous, what a dainty painted kaleidoscope of colour on your silky-satin wings!"

"That's true," said the butterfly, gazing at her beautiful wings, and then looking down at Pelik in disdain. "And you are so… blobby, so knobbly and stubbly, a blot on my landscape, a pitiful sight. Go hide in a dark place until it is night. Be gone now, take flight!"

If anyone said that to me, Dearly Beloved— well, you already know what I would do, but as you know, Pelik was different. No matter what unkind words were used of Pelik, she never said— or even thought—an unkind word herself.

So she wandered off, wondering whether she should try to find some small groove in the bark of a tree, where she could tuck herself up and go to sleep, not to come out again until it was dark, when she wouldn't offend any beautiful creatures.

She had not gone very far when she saw something so large, and so magnificent, that she stopped in her tracks—that is to say, in her flight—and fell to the ground with a very small thud. She had landed on the edge of a large puddle. The huge and beautiful thing stopped in its tracks also, and looked about it. Then, to Pelik's amazement, it gave itself a little shake and spread out its tail like a gigantic fan. It was so enormous that Pelik couldn't see anything above it, or below it, or on either side of it. Our little beetle's whole world was filled with the iridescent greens and blues and goldy-bronze colours of the creature's tail.

She gazed at it in wonder. "Oh most wonderful Burung Merak," she said (for that is the word for 'peacock' in Malay), "your feathers bejewelled like a precious tiara, its splendour endlessly emerald!"

The peacock looked all about him. "That's true," he said, gazing at his reflection in the puddle, and preening himself proudly. Then he looked around him once more. "But you? Who are you? And where are you?"

"Why, surely you can see me, oh mighty Burung Merak," Pelik said in surprise, "for you have more eyes on your streaming, gleaming, shimmering tail than I have ever seen."

This was true, Best Beloved, for a peacock's tail is covered in patterns which look just like eyes.

"But perhaps," Pelik said sadly, "you cannot see me because I am so very insignificant. I am brown and ugly and very, very small. I am on the ground at your feet."

The peacock peered at the ground until he saw Pelik's tiny eye glinting in the sunlight.

"I am on my way to hide in a dark place until it is night," Pelik explained, "so that I don't spoil the butterfly's view. Or the dragonfly's view. Or your view, come to that."

"But why should you hide?" the peacock asked, looking at her curiously. "It is true that you are ugly, but you have as much right to the sunlight as anyone else. And in any case, there isn't any point in hiding yourself away this afternoon." He tipped his head to one side and sniffed the air. "A storm to end all storms is coming. The butterfly and the dragonfly will be hiding themselves—they may be beautiful (in a very small way, of course)," he added, glancing again at his own impressive reflection, "but they are fragile. They do not have your leathery wings. They cannot cope with heavy rain. And as for spoiling *my* view, well…I'm afraid you are too small to matter to *me*."

If anyone said that to me, Dearly Beloved—

well, you already know my views on that subject, but since the peacock had been a great deal more polite than the other creatures, I shall let him off. And, as you know, Pelik was different. No matter what unkind words were used of Pelik, she never said—or even thought—an unkind word herself.

So she continued on her way, a little heartened by the words of the wise peacock, and heading this time for the big, black clouds which were gathering on the horizon. She had not gone very far when the first fat blobs of rain began to fall, bouncing off her leathery wings and exploding on the ground. The jungle grew very still and quiet, and very, very dark. Then a sound as loud as fifty tigers bounced from tree to tree, shaking Pelik, who was quaking with fright. She had never heard thunder before, and she hid at the top of a tree, in case it could gobble her up.

When she had reached the very top of the tallest tree she could see the whole sky. Thunder was rolling around, first from one direction, then another. Then suddenly the whole sky was lit up by a streak of lightning which tore the sky in two. A deafening clap of thunder burst above Pelik's head, and her mouth opened in wonder. A sudden hot, sharp, flaming heat filled her like a fire. The rain was drumming on her back like a thousand slaps. She sat there, looking at the sky in amazement. Then, gradually, the rain drops slowed, the thunder rumbled away, and the sky cleared. Soon steam was rising from the puddles which covered the jungle floor, and frogs began to croak, birds began to sing, and large leaves dripped wetly on to the ground.

Pelik shook herself dry, then flew up into the air. She was far from home, and her mother would worry if she wasn't home before nightfall. She flew and flew, watching the sun sink below the horizon. Soon the jungle would be pitch black, and she would have difficulty finding her way. Pelik flew faster and faster. And yet, strangely, it didn't seem to be getting any darker: there was always a little light around her. The night was dark, O Best Beloved, but not absolutely black. Then, when she was nearly home, Pelik flew over a puddle—the storm had left a lot of puddles—and she saw the reflection of a gleam, a little glimmer, a tiny shiny glistening winking blinking light, right where she was flying. It must be the reflection of a star, she thought, and flew on. It was dark—and then not so dark. Dark—and then not so dark.

She could hear her brothers and sisters, and mother and father, her uncles and aunts all calling, long before she reached her home. "Kelip-kelip!"

they were shouting, "Kelip-kelip!"

"I haven't been gone that long," she said, as she landed amongst them, "Have you forgotten my name? I'm Pelik, not Kelip!"

But they took no notice. "Kelip-kelip!" they said, delightedly, for 'kelip' means 'to twinkle' in Malay, and that is just what Pelik was doing.

Over the next few weeks, everyone watched Pelik carefully, wondering when her light would go out. But it didn't. Every night she glimmered and shimmered, she blinked and winked and gleamed.

The butterfly (the one with no manners) gazed at her enviously, wishing he had a bright light inside him that twinkled and flickered and danced.

The dragonfly (the one who was rude) gazed at her crossly, wondering how best to put out her light.

The peacock (the one who couldn't see her, despite his thousand eyes) took the credit for himself. "For it was I who told you that the storm was coming. You swallowed some lightning, and that is what has made you so beautiful."

"Beautiful? I'm not beautiful am I?" said Pelik (who always had beautiful thoughts, and was modest as well).

"Of course you are," the other creatures agreed

(though rather reluctantly). "From now on we shall call you 'Kelip-kelip,'" which is the Malay word for Firefly. In some countries Fireflies are called Lightning Bugs, because word got around that Kelip-kelip (as she was now called) had swallowed lightning.

But Kelip-kelip's mother would never believe it. She knew that the Kelip-keilip's light was simply her beautiful thoughts, shining out.

# How Time Learned to Be Bedtime

*Pauline J. Alama*

In a time long past—and such a long-lost time, O My Best Beloved, that Time had not begun to count the hours on his twelve fingers and twelve toes, but knew only sunrise and noon and sunset and night—there was no such thing as bedtime. Nor was there time for school, nor time for breakfast, nor time for thirty minutes of Minecraft if you finished your homework right away after school. For one thing, school hadn't been invented yet. For another thing, minutes hadn't been invented yet either. People ate when they had food, not when it was time for breakfast. And they slept—well, when they slept or didn't sleep is the matter of this story.

In that uncounted long-ago, there lived a little family of Primitive Herders.

The Papa Herdsman wore a long and flowing beard and a long and flowing name to match, which meant something like "Man Who Converses with Sheep Until He Is as Wise as One." But that is too long for everyday use, so he was called Wise for short.

The Mama Herdswoman wore long and flowing

hair and a long and flowing name to match, which meant "She Whose Wrathful Glare Would Curdle Milk Inside the Goat, But Who Is Nothing Like As Fierce As She Looks." But let us call her Fierce for short.

Now, Wise and Fierce had two small Herdschildren between them, whose long and flowing names meant "Boy Like a Monkey on a Thin Branch Who Can Never Be Still" and "Girl Whose Every Other Word is Why, Why, Why, Who Will Never Be Silent." But those names are too long for everyday use, so we'll call them Still and Silent.

They did not have many things, these Primitive Herders. They didn't have Wii or DS or Xbox. They didn't have iPad or iPod or iBook. They didn't have Wi-Fi, or cable, or even an antenna on the roof (you can ask your Grandmother what that is). But they did have plenty of goats and sheep, and fortunately for them, in those days, you counted your wealth in goats and sheep, so they felt Comfortably Middle Class. The goats took grass and turned it into milk, and Fierce took the milk and turned it into cheese, and Still and Silent took the cheese and turned it into part of themselves and grew bigger and bigger. But they didn't grow a bit more Still and Silent; not even at night, when their bellies were full of good goat-milk cheese and flat bread and fruit.

One night, Wise and Fierce had put in an especially hard day of herding, and wanted very much to lie down and sleep on fleeces on the earthen floor. But they couldn't, because of all the noise coming from Still and Silent.

Despite not having Wii or DS or iPad or iPod, despite not having Minecraft or even homework to keep them up at night, Still and Silent simply would not lie down on their fleeces and sleep. They kept jumping and yelling and waking the sheep and the goats and the dogs. And what with the jumping and yelling and bleating and barking, even Time himself couldn't rest, but kept hurrying on toward another morning, when Wise and Fierce would have to rise and milk the goats all over again.

Wise, all tired and cranky from going into bramble-bushes and thorny-thickets after some silly sheep that had gotten stuck there, wisely and patiently explained that it was time for all good children to go to bed.

"Why?" said Silent.

"Because we've worked hard all day and we need to sleep."

"Why?" said Silent.

"Aren't you tired now?"

"Why?" said Silent.

"You've had a long, full day of teasing the goats and scaring the sheep and distracting the good herding-dogs. I'd think that would make anyone ready to sleep." And Wise yawned a great yawn, and the dogs that lay across the doorway yawned in sympathy.

"But I'm not tired, Papa!" shouted Still, bouncing up and down to show how wide awake he was. The goats in their pen heard the commotion and stamped and bleated, and the dogs roused and barked at them to be quiet and go to sleep.

"Even if you're not ready to sleep, lie down now anyway," said Wise, not quite so patiently as before.

"But why, Papa? WHY?" asked Silent.

"BECAUSE I SAID SO!" snapped Wise, then he stomped off and told Fierce she'd better have a try.

Fierce came in, all tired and cranky from pounding up herbs to make salve for the sores of the beasts that had gone into the bramble-bush. "Have you bad kids been giving your poor father trouble? You'd better go to sleep RIGHT NOW." She glared her most dreadful glare, the one that could curdle the milk inside the goat. But Still kept right on bouncing about like a monkey on a branch, and Silent said, "But why, Mama? Why?" And they kept it up no matter how she glared, because they knew she was Nothing Like as Fierce as She Looked.

They were right, of course. Instead of spanking the children, Fierce sat down beside them on the earthen floor. "Aren't these fleeces soft? Why don't you lie down by me and listen to a story. Listen to me, O my best beloved children. In the high and far-off times, the goat had no horn."

"Why?" said Silent.

"I was just about to tell you," said Fierce, "if you'd only lie down quietly and listen. In those days there was a kid goat, a curious little fellow, full of 'satiable curiosity."

"Why?" said Silent.

"All day long, he asked why, why, why."

"Why?" said Silent.

"I don't know. Why do you do it?" Fierce began to forget what story she'd been about to tell. She yawned a great yawn, and the herding dogs that lay across the doorway all yawned in sympathy.

Still decided this meant the dogs needed another game of tug-of-war, and ran over to rouse them up. The dogs barked, and the sheep woke and bleated at them to shut up for once and let them sleep.

"Oh, I give up!" Glaring her most ferocious glare, Fierce stomped out.

"Where are you going, Fierce?" her husband said fearfully.

"I'm going to get help from my aunt," she said. "My aunt will know what to do."

Now, She Whose Wrathful Glare Would Curdle Milk Inside the Goat, But Who Is Nothing Like As Fierce As She Looks had an old aunt who had helped to raise her, who lived alone just a little way up the hill. This aunt had sharp, bright eyes that made Man Who Converses With Sheep Till He is As Wise as One feel that she saw him all too clearly, and a sharp, long nose that made him feel she smelled something fishy about him, and a sharp, loud voice that made him feel he'd better do what she said or suffer the consequences. He called this formidable old woman "My Wife's Aunt, Which Is the Scariest Woman In Three Tribes." But as that was too long for everyday use, she was most often known as Aunt Which, or Aunt Witch.

Aunt Witch came down the hill, leaning on her walking stick, and Wise shuddered at the sight of her, and even the goats grew wary at the sound of her stick tap-tap-tapping its way down the path.

But the dogs at the doorway of the herdsman's hut wagged their tails, while Still and Silent jumped up to dance around her, shouting and laughing. Aunt Witch scratched the dogs behind the ears, and she hugged her grandnephew and grandniece, and then she spoke to them in her sharp, clear voice: "What's this I hear that you won't go to sleep?"

"We're not sleepy," said Still, dancing around her.

"Why should we lie down when we're not sleepy?" sang out Silent.

"You're going to lie down," said Aunt Witch in her sharp, clear voice that brooked no contradictions, "and you're going to lie still, and you're going to be quiet and listen to me. Because if you aren't still, and if you aren't quiet, you won't hear this song I'm going to sing, which is a song like no other you've ever heard, a song is especially for you, my darling Still and my beloved Silent. Listen!" And she began to sing to them:

*Let all your wakefulness flee from your eyes*

*Let all your fidgets take wing with the flies*

*Let all your jumpiness fly out the door*

*While you sleep in peace on your fleece on the*

*floor*

*Let all your wakefulness fly up the hill*

*And leave sleeping children, Silent and Still*

*Let all your fidgets fly up the hill*

*And leave sleeping children, Silent and Still*

*Let all your jumpiness fly up the hill*

*And leave sleeping children, Silent and Still*

*Let all your chattering fly up the hill*

*And leave sleeping children, Silent and Still*

So Aunt Witch sang, first clear and loud, then softer and softer, over and over, and that was the first lullaby. It was also a spell, because Aunt Witch wasn't called Aunt Witch for nothing. And because her song was a spell and an incantation, the dogs lay down across the doorway, the children laid their heads on the soft fleeces, and the fidgets and jumpiness and chatter and wide-awakeness left their bodies and flew out the door and up the hill. The two children drowsed and dreamed, and like all children, they looked perfectly angelic while asleep. Then Wise and Fierce thanked Aunt Witch a thousand times, and they too settled down and slept. And Aunt Witch, all tired out from the mighty spell she had cast, lay down next to the children and fell asleep. And even Time finally realized it was Bedtime, and dozed a little to let them all rest.

But the awakeness and the fidgets and the jumpiness and the chattering that had left the children had to go somewhere. They might have settled in the goats, except that Aunt Witch had commanded them up the hill, so up the hill they went. But they hadn't gotten far before they got caught in the branches of a bush that grew on the hillside. The bush was full of green berries, and a fidget or a jump or a chatter or a wide-eyed-wake-up settled into every little berry on that bush and turned them all wide-awake red.

The next morning, Fierce awoke from a blessedly unbroken sleep. She saw that her husband was sleeping, and her children were sleeping, and her old aunt from up the hill was sleeping, but she knew the goats would need to be milked, so she went about the milking by herself. And while she carried the milking pail out to the pen, still dreamy and groggy in the morning mist, she happened to cast her eyes up the hill and see a shrub covered with bright little berries all wide-awake red.

She felt a bit hungry, so she picked one of the red berries, popped it in her mouth—and coughed with surprise. Her eyes popped wide open, and

Fierce looked fiercer than ever, because all her children's wide-awakeness had gone into those berries. Now wide, wide awake, she set about milking the goats with a will.

When she returned to the hut, she found her husband and her aunt and her children Still and Silent still asleep. It seemed high time for Wise to get up tend the flocks, so she took another of the berries off the wide-awake tree and popped it in his mouth. He coughed with shock and bounced up off his fleece, because Silent's noise and chatter and Still's jump and jitter had gone into that berry. And the noise he made woke Still and Silent and Aunt Witch.

The first thing Aunt Witch said was, "What's that cough-ey noise I hear?

And so the bush that took the children's wide-awakeness at night has been called "coffee" ever since. Aunt Witch learned to brew its berries into a potion that gives grown-ups all the wide-awakeness children have before bedtime. And even to this day, Best Beloved, you may see your Mama and Papa use that brew, so full of fidgets and jumps and wide-awakeness, to wake up in the morning. But don't drink it yourself, please: you have quite enough natural wide-awakeness of your own.

# Mind Your P's and Q's

*Robert Walden*

I expect you know your alphabet, little one. The alphabet starts like this: 'a,' 'b,' 'c'… and ends 'x,' 'y,' 'z.' Now, the alphabet is the beginning of all things pertaining to words, for when you regard words properly (which you always should), you will see that letters of the alphabet make up every word. You may also know that you must place these letters in a specific order for people (especially young boys and girls still attending school) to understand them. For example, the letters of the word elephant when laid side by side are: e-l-e-p-h-a-n-t. Thus, writing elephant as h-e-n-p-e-t-a-l would be quite wrong and may lead to considerable confusion. Spelling is the name given to placing letters in the correct order inside a word. What you may not know (probably because no one has ever told you) is why we call this particular practice spelling. Actually, the elephant and the hippopotamus, and indeed all animals (who are now renowned for their meticulous spelling) are responsible.

Spelling started with an argument!

In fairness to the animals involved, the now infamous argument was more a heated debate—between the elephant and anyone who cared to engage him (mostly no one since the elephant was so large and frankly, quite scary when he got riled). This argument started a long, long time ago when animals (especially animal young and cubs who are always curious creatures) first started to think about words and reading and how useful books would be if only they existed (which of course they didn't such a long, long time ago). Around this time, the letters of the alphabet were wild and untamed (more so even than the animals).

Like fidgeting children, letters would not stay still for long, making collecting a complete alphabet difficult. Some letters lived on high mountains (those that didn't mind great heights and steep alpine slopes, like the letters 'h' and 'l'). Some lived on the Great Plains and savannahs (those that liked to run and jump with freedom like the letters 'r' and 'z'). Some lived in the seas, rivers and great lakes (those that liked bathing and swimming and generally messing about in water, like the letters 'f' and 'w'). Some lived in hot climates close to the equator (those that could stand the oppressive heat and loved sunning themselves, like the letters 'o' and 's'). Some lived in extremely cold climates near the North and South poles (those that didn't mind the freezing snow and ice, like the letters 'i' and 'g'), and so forth. The great animal explorers of the day had even spotted difficult to find letters like the timid 'j' deep in the inaccessible jungles of the Amazon. In truth, letters were running free and wild all over the globe. In fact, if one made a list of all known letters (which no one had thought to do except the famed golden-breasted owl, who knew the preferred habitats of most letters), only the whereabouts of the elusive letters 'p' and 'q' remained a mystery—even to the learned strigiform.

Nevertheless, the animal young and cubs (who long ago used to play nicely together) set about catching letters in their butterfly nets (for ancient letters were extremely fluttery creatures) and they began making the first words, starting with their names (which always seems like a good place to start writing). Words like elehant, which is what the long trunked pachyderm was originally called until one day he paused while spraying cooling water and mud from the Lamboozo river long enough to complain to anyone who would listen.

"That's not fair!" he would trumpet. "I'm not an elehant. My name has a 'ph' in it", and he made a 'ph' sound by putting his tongue between his teeth, like this. "How can I write a 'ph' sound without the letter 'p'? Something must be done!" The elehant stamped his feet making the ground rumble (though thankfully he did not have a full tantrum, which was something to behold and dangerous to smaller creatures).

"You could use two 'f's", suggested a smug looking flamingo wading close by (who didn't have any trouble spelling his name correctly). "There are plenty swimming about in the river. Look! There they go!" Quick as a flash the elehant schlooped up a trunk full of water and mud (and several letter 'f's in the process) and sprayed them on the muddy riverbank, thereby stranding the captured letters. He promptly gathered the floundering 'f's and set about writing his name in the mud as the smug flamingo had suggested (using two 'f's instead of the missing letter 'p'), like this: e-l-e-f-f-h-a-n-t.

"I don't know," said the puzzled long-nosed fellow staring at the word despondently and mouthing the letter sounds. "It sounds better, but it still isn't right!"

"No it isn't," said another small-eared pachyderm who had been lurking hidden in the muddy waters and who had listened to the elehant's complaint with keen interest. This stout beast had more right to complain even than the elehant for the huge creature was what we now correctly call the hippopotamus, but back then incorrectly was known as the hiootamus, a name that our wallowing friend found distasteful because the lack of 'p's undermined his status as the master of the waterways.

"Then what shall I do?" asked the eleffhant (temporarily changing his name until a permanent solution could be found).

The hiootamus flapped his small ears. "I suggest that unless all animals can spell their names correctly that we cancel words and writing completely." He flapped his ears again trying to dislodge a bothersome letter u jittering about his head. "These fluttering letters are a pain to catch at the best of times and even then they won't stay put. And we've done without reading and writing until now, so why should we bother?"

"But you can't!" cried the other animals, most of whom could spell their names easily and were looking forward to moving on to other words.

"Perhaps we could ban a few common letters to even matters," buzzed the hornet. "The letters 'f' and 'g' perhaps?"

"That's not fair," snapped the flamingo,

suddenly not looking quite so smug. He had no desire for everyone to call him a lamino. "Why not lose the letter 'h'?" he said in retaliation.

The potentially named ornet buzzed angrily. Other animals joined the small group already in heated debate, each offering their own suggestions of which letters they should lose. Soon the meeting turned into debacle with several animals engaging in the ancient art of argy-bargee. (Which was definitely not playing nicely!)

"Stop!" The command was said with such authority that for a moment all the animals froze, fearing they had disturbed the lion, who was without doubt the undisputed king of all animals and didn't take kindly to being disturbed. Luckily the lion was on the other side of the prairie trying to run down a letter 'z' that so far had stayed tantalisingly just out of reach of the great beast's net. No one had noticed the golden-breasted owl high in the top of the willow-wallow tree, watching the proceedings with interest and more than a little impatience.

The owl was the first animal to learn to read and write and everyone regarded him as the ultimate authority on letters. Perhaps you have heard of the wise old owl. Well, the owl is wise for many reasons, not least because he has been reading the longest of all creatures. "It is clear to me," he said, "that the only way to resolve this matter is to find the elusive letters 'p' and 'q.'"

This was great in theory, but not so easy in practice.

"Where shall we look?" asked the gathered animals.

"I know many things, but that I do not know," admitted the owl, "but we must search high and we must search low until we find them both. I suggest all animals split into teams and work together until we are successful." The animals looked at each other in bewilderment. They had never worked together in teams before. Traditionally they had strived alone, following the edict of the wild known as the survival of the fittest, which is why animals, unlike humans, take exercise so seriously. That is, except for the cat, which had always been lazy and rebellious and relied instead on guile and luck.

However, the animals thought working together worth a try, so they split into teams and set about searching the far reaches of the globe for the elusive letters. After years of searching the highest mountains and the deepest ravines, the widest seas and the longest rivers without success, the animals returned to the watering hole abject and defeated.

They reported to the owl, which in their absence had been learning animal magic and conducting experiments on the best way to tame and preserve letters.

"We have searched everywhere," the animals bemoaned. "It is time to give up our quest."

"There is one place we haven't looked—the caves of Kilimanjaro!" The animals looked shocked. Even the mighty lion had turned a peculiar shade of green, because Kilimanjaro was the last resting place of the dragons. Dragons were ancient creatures that preferred peace and quiet in their old age. They did not mix well with other animals and resented them for their youth and energy.

"Still, someone should go," repeated the owl. "I cannot for my wings make too much noise."

"I cannot," said the eleffhant, "for my footfall is too loud."

One by one, each animal gave an excuse why he shouldn't be the one to go to the dreaded caves, until only the timid mouse hadn't spoken. All eyes turned toward him. For the first time the mouse felt noticed and important. He gathered all his courage.

"I'll go," he said, puffing out his little furry chest with pride. "Though, someone will have to take me to the mountain for my little legs are made for scurrying not travelling great distances."

"I will carry you in my beak," replied the golden-breasted owl, "and wait outside the caves to carry you back." The owl carried the timid mouse in his hooked beak to the fabled mountain (not once thinking about swallowing the mouse for his lunch because the little creature was on such important business). Once on the mountain, the great owl blinked and set the mouse on his way. "Good luck, little fellow."

Inside the caves, the mouse discovered the ancient dragons snoozing on their hordes of treasure (treasure being as comfortable as a soft mattress to dragons). First, the mouse searched the caves, scurrying as quietly as he could around the edges. When he did not find any letters, there was nowhere to look other than the treasure. He crept as quietly as he could (which was amazingly quiet even for a tiny mouse) towards the sleeping beasts, but to his great dismay the nearest dragon opened one great eye and stared at him down his long nose. A little puff of smoke escaped from his flaring nostrils when he yawned. The dragon still had all his jagged teeth the mouse noticed, teeth that could grind his tiny bones with the greatest of ease.

"Hello little creature," the dragon said. "Who or

what are you?"

The mouse puffed out his chest once more, much to the great dragon's amusement. "I'm a mouse."

"Well, proud little mouse, what do you want that is so important you would dare disturb my sleep?"

"I'm on a quest for letters. 'P' and 'q' especially."

"A quest eh? Aren't you a little small to go questing?" growled the dragon, knotting his eyebrows. "What are these letters you hope to find?"

"Little fluttery creatures, my lord."

"Fluttery, you say. I was wondering what those were." The dragon lifted one great leg and underneath in two glass boxes with silver handles were the 'p's and 'q's. The dragon handed a box to the mouse. "Take this with my blessing, mouse. Letters, eh? Well, they are far too active for my liking. Now go and leave me in peace!" With that, the dragon closed his eyes and was asleep in seconds.

The mouse dragged the glass box containing the 'q's outside to the waiting owl. The great golden-breasted owl looked on the mouse with a new sense of admiration. "Was it dangerous inside the caves?"

"I'd rather not talk about my ordeal," replied the mouse, which was true for the less he said, the more he left to the owl's imagination, and after all, he had been brave to enter the caves when no one else would.

"Did you see any 'p's," asked the owl.

"I believe I did." Relieved of his burden the mouse scurried back towards the cave entrance.

"You mean to go back inside a second time?"

"Yes," shouted the mouse over his shoulder. "Why not?"

"Well, I'll take the box of 'q's back to the clearing and come back for you. Take care, brave fellow."

Once again inside the caves, the mouse crept as quickly as he could towards the sleeping dragons and the hordes of treasure that he knew contained the letter 'p's. Again, to his dismay the nearest dragon opened one great eye and spied his approach. (In fairness to the mouse, the dragon was acting as guard sentry and was on particular alert for intruders.)

"You again," growled the dragon, a little irritated at being disturbed again so soon.

"Yes, me, the harmless little mouse."

"Annoying little mouse, more like. On another

quest?"

"The same quest, my lord. Remember those fluttery creatures. I was wondering if I could take the second glass box."

"Ungrateful little fellow, aren't you. Not satisfied with one box, eh?"

"Not ungrateful, my lord. Thankful. I appreciate your kindness, for your generosity is well known throughout the animal kingdom."

"Animals have a kingdom now do they? Well, I suppose it was inevitable one day. The time of dragons is over and they will soon be forgotten."

The quick-thinking mouse formulated an idea. "Not forgotten, my lord. Animals are learning to read and write, which is why we need the fluttery creatures. We could write of the great dragon dynasties for everyone to read and remember."

"You could do that?"

"I believe so."

"Then I will gladly give you the second box. Now, will you leave me in peace?"

The mouse answered quietly that he would, but the dragon was already asleep. The mouse dragged the glass box containing the letter 'p's outside to the waiting owl. The owl's admiration for the little mouse turned into awe.

"Well, brave little mouse, it's time I took you

home." He carried the glass box and the mouse to the clearing by the watering hole, where the other animals were waiting eagerly. Like the owl, all the animals held the little mouse with new regard. He was exalted far and wide for his courage. Even the eleffant was nervous of the new hero (and remains so to this day). Only the cat (which had been asleep throughout the great search and the mouse's adventure) did not hold the mouse in awe and today continues to chase and tease the mouse much as he ever had—but then cats are a law unto themselves.

At last, all animals could spell their names correctly. The eleffhant got his p and now spells his name e-l-e-p-h-a-n-t, as did the hiootamus (three actually) and can now write his name with pride as h-i-p-p-o-p-o-t-a-m-u-s and even lesser animals such as the uail got a letter q to become q-u-a-i-l.

Though the animals finally had collected all the letters of the alphabet, there remained the problem of retaining them, for, being wild and carefree, the letters had a tendency to flutter off, leaving unsightly gaps in words. As usual, the animals turned to the great golden-breasted owl for guidance. Thankfully, he had almost perfected his experiments. He knew how to cure the letters of their wildness and their desire constantly to flutter. Almost—even then, he had to use magic to keep them in place, which is why we now call arranging letters correctly in words spelling. Today, letters are domesticated and for the most part, they behave. Occasionally, they go missing or change position in words when they should know better. That is particularly so for the letters 'p' and 'q,' which being the last letters captured remain the wildest, which is why you may hear the expression "to mind your 'p's and 'q's," for if not watched they still tend to go wandering.

What of the brave little mouse? The furry fellow kept his promise and wrote the definitive work on the history of the great dragon clans, which is how we know of dragons today even though they no longer exist. Sometimes (if you remain absolutely quiet) you will hear a mouse scurrying from room to room or you may hear the tiny scratching as he writes in his journal. Of all his great works, the mouse has never written of his adventure inside the dragon caves, nor has he told another living soul, which is why you and I must keep what happened a secret!

# The Nidibalan

*Patricia S. Bowne*

A long, long time ago, when there were only a few families in the valley, this man was walking in the forest. He passed the Nidibalan, which was hunting in the form of a rat with whiskers three times as long as its body. It followed after the man until he sat down against a tree and yawned. Then it jumped out of its rat body into his mouth, and hid at the base of his throat.

When the man went home, his wife set out supper before him and their children. The Nidibalan in his throat opened its jaws wide, and its whiskers stood out of the man's mouth. Before his children could even cry out, the Nidibalan had eaten all the food. The family went to bed hungry.

At midnight, the man opened his mouth and began to snore. The Nidibalan crawled out and went into the kitchen. There it ate and ate, until the sun came over the horizon. At the first sign of light, it ran back into the man's throat. But it left not a grain of food in the house.

"We have nothing!" the man's wife said to him. "What will the children eat?"

The man opened his mouth. He wanted to tell his wife that he would care for them. But the

Nidibalan spoke out of his mouth. "Eh, woman, stop bothering me!" it said. "What kind of wife cannot cook for her husband? I will have to go somewhere else for what I need." The man did not know what to do, for he could not say what he wished to. He ran out of the house and left his wife crying.

Two compounds down, the man's sister was setting out breakfast for her family. "Eh, brother," she called when she saw the man walk by. "What brings you out this early? Stop and drink tea with us."

The man opened his mouth to refuse, but the Nidibalan inside him opened its jaws wide until its whiskers stood out of his mouth. Before anybody could so much as speak, it ate up everything on the table. "Eh, woman," it said, "that was nothing near enough. What kind of family puts such scraps on the table for hungry men? I will have to go elsewhere for what I need."

The man was ashamed, and could not say what he wished to say. He ran away in the forest. All day he wandered there, and whatever he came near, the Nidibalan ate up: fruits and plants, deer and rabbits.

Back in the village, the man's sister ran to see his wife. "What's become of my brother!" she cried, and shared her story. They did not know what to think.

But the sister said, "We must ask Banyan Woman."

Banyan Woman was older than the village. She lived alone in the banyan tree beside the clearing, and knew more than any other person. The women went to her and told their story, and she listened. "This is the Nidibalan," she said. "This has moved into your husband. You are lucky that you fed it last night, because if you had not, it would have stayed awake and made love to you, and then you would never get it out of him again.

"Now you must cook for it again tonight, ten times as much as you cooked last night, but when it comes to the table put garbage upon the plates, and hide the good food in the kitchen. Make sure you give it enough garbage to fill its stomach, so it sleeps well. Then at midnight when your husband begins to snore, the Nidibalan will wake and run out of his mouth into the kitchen, to eat the good food. Tie your husband's mouth shut with a cloth, and the Nidibalan will not be able to go back into him. When the sun rises, it will have to go into the creature nearest it."

"But what will that be?" the man's wife asked.

"Whatever you have put there," said Banyan

Woman. "But be sure you are not in the house at sunrise, or it will go into you."

The wife went home and set a snare out beside the dikes, to catch the smallest thing she could catch. She cooked all the food she could borrow. She put it into the kitchen, hidden behind pots on the shelves. Then she loaded the table with garbage, old bones and rotten fruits. When she ran back to the snare, she had caught a short-tailed shrew smaller than her middle finger: she tied it in her overscarf and went back into the house.

Just then her husband came home, looking sad. He wanted to tell her what had happened to him, but when he opened his mouth the Nidibalan said "Woman, is this all you can give me? This is barely enough for half a man." And it gobbled up all the garbage. Then the man lay down on the bed and fell into a deep sleep.

The woman sent her children to their aunt's house and cleaned the kitchen. She took the little shrew out of her scarf and put it into a teapot, and hid the teapot in the rafters of the kitchen. Then she went to bed and waited until midnight.

At midnight her husband opened his mouth and began to snore. The woman watched from under her eyelids as the Nidibalan crawled out of his mouth with its whiskers trailing behind it. It ran into the kitchen, and there it began to eat up the food. But as soon as it was gone, the woman took a long strip of cloth and tied it around her husband's face, under his jaw and up to the top of his head. She tied his mouth shut. Then she ran out of the house.

The Nidibalan ate and ate in the kitchen, until the sun was almost up. It ran back to the bed, but the man's mouth was tied tight shut. The Nidibalan ran all around the house, searching for something to go into. Then it heard scratching from the rafters of the kitchen, where the shrew was trying to get out of the teapot. The Nidibalan jumped into the shrew's mouth, just as the sun beamed into the kitchen.

When the woman came back into the kitchen and looked into the teapot, she could see the Nidibalan's long whiskers sticking out of the shrew's mouth. "Eh," she said, "you will not get out again!" She grasped the whiskers and tied them around the shrew's tail, so they trailed behind. That's how the shrew got its long tail. The Nidibalan struggled and fought, but there was no way for it to get out of the shrew.

Some say that the Nidibalan was so ashamed when it found itself trapped in a shrew that it ran out of the valley to a far country, all the way to the

king's court. The king cut the tail off of the shrew
with his sword, and the Nidibalan ran out and leapt
inside him. But we say the Nidibalan is still inside
the shrew, and that is why the shrew eats more
than any other creature. No other animal will eat
the shrew, because they are all glad to have the
Nidibalan where they can keep an eye on it. Our
people will never molest the shrew that carries the
Nidibalan and keeps us safe from it. So if you see a
shrew, give it something to eat. But not too much
and not too good, or it will follow you home. And
who knows what might happen at midnight?

# The Fruit Tree

*Arthur Powers*

You have heard, Loved One, of the Garden of
Eden and of Adam and Eve, whom God put there.
You know that it was a beautiful place, filled with
flowers and green plants, and trees standing in the
sunlight, laden with richly colored fruit. There
were animals, too—gentle, peaceful animals who
lived quietly, eating the fruit and the plentiful
grasses. But perhaps you have not heard of the
special place in Eden of the Dog and the Cat.

Those two were the special servants of Adam
and Eve. Who can say why God made them so?
Perhaps He desired that Man and Woman know
something of the duties of masterhood. For, just as
Adam and Eve were perfect servants to God, Dog
and Cat were perfect servants to them.

While both animals were servants to both, it
happened that Dog most closely attended upon
Adam, and Cat upon Eve. When Adam ran down
among the wilder parts of the Garden, breathing
the sharp air and pretending—even then—that
everything was his, Dog would run with him. And
when Eve walked in the orchard, feeling the good,
warm sunlight on her skin and enjoying the bright

colors of the flowers, Cat would walk with her.

Eve was a beautiful woman with long, dark hair and deep, clear eyes. Age had not touched her and could not touch her, and she knew nothing of worry or pain. She sang sweetly and laughed gently; she was warm and tender and kind. And she loved Adam strongly.

By day she and Adam were sometimes together, sometimes apart. At night they slept in each other's arms. But always they loved—sleeping, waking, together, apart—loved with a thoughtless and innocent love that had always been and would always be. They laughed and ran and explored, showing things to one another. She was perfection to him, and he was perfection to her.

Early one morning, Eve was walking slowly among the fruit trees. Cat was with her, playing at her heels. He chased her feet and rubbed against her leg, rolled up into a ball, unwound, and leapt at flowers. Then, running up onto the low branches of a fruit tree, he touched her cheek with his soft paw.

"Oh, Cat!" Eve laughed. "You *are* a funny animal."

Cat said nothing, for Cats do not talk. But he was pleased—he loved his mistress and it made him happy to amuse her.

Now, in all the Garden, there was only one tree whose fruit God had forbidden Adam and Eve and the animals to eat. Wandering that morning, Eve and Cat came within sight of that tree. The sun, rising just a little above the tops of the smaller trees, seemed to beam particularly on that one, and morning dew glistened on the fruit. That fruit, Loved One—how can I describe it? Imagine the finest fruit you know, a dozen times lovelier—the most beautiful color, a dozen times richer—and changing, as the day and your mood change, always inviting, always delectable. This was the fruit that Eve saw as she walked in the orchard that morning.

She came close to it, and leaned against a nearby pear tree. Cat climbed up onto a branch of the pear tree so that he was close beside her shoulder. He savored the quiet morning, and purred.

Eve stood looking at the fruit a long time. The sun climbed higher and the fruit glistened, always changing, always delectable. Once she said:

"It *is* beautiful, Cat, isn't it?"

Cat said nothing, for Cats do not talk. But he purred and waved his tail.

She had no thought of touching or tasting the fruit. She just looked on, delighted. The sun climbed higher in the sky, and the fruit glistened, always inviting, always changing.

"It *is* beautiful, Eve, isn't it?"

Her own words, almost echoed, in a soft, hissing voice. She took her eyes from the fruit and looked around for the speaker. On a nearby branch she saw Snake, green and glittering, lying in the sunshine, his eyes half closed.

"Yes, Snake," she said. "It is."

Cat looked and also saw Snake, and yet he purred. For neither he nor his mistress knew anything of Evil.

Time passed and the sun grew hotter, and the fruit glistened even more brightly before Snake said:

"It is indeed beautiful to look at, very beautiful. But that is nothing compared to its touch."

Eve was surprised. "You've touched it, Snake?"

"Many times," he said, "and its touch is more wonderful than its beauty."

"But surely it is forbidden," she said.

"Forbidden?" he said, "to touch it?" He fully opened one eye. "Surely it is not forbidden to touch it. To touch is not to taste."

But she was afraid, and she said: "I will not touch it."

"Ah, do not," the Snake answered, "though to

touch it is wonderful beyond imagination and can do no harm. But I wish you could feel it once, for the feeling is greater than the beauty. Go close to it, at least, and look."

She left the pear tree and took two steps closer to the fruit—coming close enough to reach out and touch it if she wanted to. The fruit gleamed before her eyes.

"Oh, how can anything so beautiful do harm?"

"It can't," said the Snake. "Touch it."

Almost in spite of herself she reached up her hand and touched the fruit. It was wonderful: soft and firm and thrilling to her fingers. More wonderful than its beauty. She reached up her other hand and held the fruit between the two.

Time passed, and the Snake was silent while Eve held the fruit and looked at it, smiling, feeling thrilled and deeply happy. Cat still reclined on his bough, half asleep, purring and waving his tail.

After a while Eve said, "It is very wonderful."

"It's getting late," Snake said. "Noon has passed."

"Yes," she answered, taking no real notice.

There was a silence. Snake said, "It is wonderful to touch and see, very wonderful. But it is much more wonderful to taste."

She hardly glanced at him, but smiled. "You

haven't tasted it, Snake."

"Many times," he answered, "and its succulence is greater than its beauty and its touch."

"How could you have tasted it?" she asked, looking at him now. "It is forbidden."

"To taste is not to eat."

"Ah! But it *is*, Snake," she said.

"Perhaps," he answered. "But I have tasted it and I am here. Do you think God has time to watch each small thing we do?"

"I don't know." She looked back at the fruit, confused. "It's forbidden."

"And why forbidden?" he asked. "Can such a beautiful thing do harm?"

"Surely it can't," she said. She turned toward him and, as she did, her hands on the fruit plucked it from the tree. She held it and looked at it.

"Then why forbidden?" he hissed, his voice intense. "Is it because He wishes to keep the sweetest fruit and the best for Himself? He, in His grand selfishness?"

"No. Surely not."

Another silence. The Snake's voice was gentle again.

"It is late, Eve. Noon has passed. Will you have a pear? An apple? A peach?"

She felt then the gnawing in her stomach. She

looked at the nearby trees and saw the fruits on them—small and pale and ugly. She knew that they would feel harsh, that they would taste bitter. Her eyes returned to the fruit in her hands.

"How can something so beautiful do harm?" Snake asked.

Slowly she raised the beautiful fruit to her mouth, and slowly she took a bite of it. And it was sweet—succulent and full-flavored—as she took her first and only taste.

For Cat, Cat who knew nothing of Evil, leapt suddenly from his branch, and with teeth and claws tore the fruit from her hands and mouth, tumbling with it to the ground.

Then Eve looked down at Cat, who stood over the fallen fruit like its predator. She saw that the ground beneath the Cat was stone, and that the light was dimmed. And looking up, she saw she was in a cave, gray light entering at one end. All the Garden was gone, and only the Cat and the fruit had come with her from Eden.

She looked down again at the Cat and she said, "Oh Cat! What have I done?" And he was silent and he crouched, looking at her and guarding the fruit. And she said, "Oh Cat, you must understand. I cannot do this alone. I cannot be here alone. I must find Adam."

She stooped down and reached for the fruit. And the Cat, who might have fought for it, did not. She picked it up and ran out into the gray light, into the barren world, to find the Man. And soon he came, and she saw that he was not perfect, but she loved him. And she gave him the fruit to eat—one bite before she seized it and hurled it far away.

Then he, too, saw—and he was afraid. And he knew that never again would they be perfect servants to God. And he loved her.

So they were cast out, eastward from Eden. With them went the Dog and the Cat.

Some people say the Dog never knew—that, though he suffered from his master's fall, though he was hurt and wondering, he was always loyal, waiting to return to Eden.

But the Cat, Loved One. The Cat, when he seized the fruit, ate a tiny bit of it, caught it in his clasping teeth. Oh, not as much as Man and Woman, but enough. So that even today he knows there is Evil in the world, and even today he can never be a perfect servant.

# Gravity's Final Hug

*Russ Bickerstaff*

It was a very long time ago. Before the world wide web. Before cities and farms and organisms coughing up for the first time on beaches. It was before beaches, in fact. So suffice it to say, it was very, very long time ago. It was a time long before Gravity became the kind of responsible force of nature you and I know it as. Back then, Gravity didn't pull firmly to the ground for everyone. Back then, Gravity was far more impetuous than anyone can possibly imagine. Listen closely and you might hear the Wind whispering about those old days before Gravity became what it is today.

Contrary to what one might think, Gravity isn't some cold, uncaring force that pulls everything to the ground, quite often causing planes and buildings and people to fall to the earth with catastrophically unhealthy impacts. Gravity feels quite a bit of remorse whenever this happens, but quite often it's far too excited about loving everything to notice when some of its love causes things to fall apart. As tragic as this state of affairs is, it's not really anywhere near as bad as it had been long ago before the world wide web and cities and beaches and things.

At the dawn of time, Gravity's love was every bit as exuberant as it is now. It would see something with some substance passing by and it would be overcome with a sense of genuine love for it. Unable to contain itself, Gravity would rush forth and embrace the object...whatever it turned out to be. Say it was a rock floating there in open space, quite happily minding its own business and enjoying a pleasant afternoon float. Out of nowhere, gravity decides to show a little affection and suddenly it's hammered to the ground unable to move.

The rocks and pebbles and things were all quite upset about this state of affairs. There had been a time where they were quite pleasant and talkative. They were very thoughtful things that would engage the clouds and the passing Wind in deep intellectual discourse. However, with gravity acting the way it had back then, they slowly grew to be in constant fear of gravity sneaking up on them and hugging them to the ground.

One day, a casual quartz mentioned to a spring breeze how frustrating it was having to deal with Gravity's constant affections. The breeze could relate. Though it was not particularly affected by Gravity, the breeze (and so many others like it)

would often find Gravity rushing by in one
direction or the other on its way to its next big hug.
Often Gravity's embrace itself might switch
directions. A wind might be casually drifting by
through a slow-moving pressure system and
suddenly there's some huge boulder passing by at
ridiculous speeds because Gravity decided that the
best way it could express its affection was by
pulling to the north with manic force.

Gravity happened to be strolling by at the time
and overheard the conversation between the casual
quartz and the spring breeze. It expressed great
concern at the fact that it would be a cause for
anyone's discomfort. The casual quartz and the
spring breeze regarded each other in silence before
returning their attentions to Gravity. The quartz
asked Gravity why it was always jumping up so
unexpectedly. Gravity slowly replied that it was
often taken with great, sweeping feelings of
affection that it felt the need to express. The quartz
explained to Gravity that the affection might feel
all the more mutual if it were able to provide some
sense of warning prior to its embrace.

Gravity considered this with a great, solemn
silence. It knew that it did not wish for its
affections to be a burden for anyone. It also knew
that it was incapable of doing anything other than

causing things to move in one direction or the other. Its force would always be constant. It could never nudge at an object by way of warning as it could only nudge as strong as it hugged.

Gravity asked the passing spring breeze if there was any way that it or any of its friends might be able to follow it around and gently blow on objects of its affection to let them know that an embrace was imminent. The breeze rocked gently, stating that wind can only react to other wind. Wind had no way of following around gravity as it was not in control of its own motions.

Gravity considered this and understood. At that moment, it felt the need to embrace the wind even though it knew it could not. Gravity *did* really need a hug at that moment, though. It enjoyed expressing its affection more than anything else in the world. How could it go on knowing that it was the cause of so much stress? It felt awful.

Knowing not what else to do, Gravity opened itself up so large that it blanketed the entire world and offered it all one big hug of apology for being so inconsiderate. It had vowed that this would be the last hug it would ever engage in, so it embraced everything indiscriminately with a gentle affection that continues to this day.

Thanks to Gravity's embrace, oceans have come

into being carrying life which has been able to swim out on land and cough up cities and advertising and the world wide web. We have accomplished all that we have in the embrace of Gravity's last hug. If people occasionally trip and buildings occasionally fall, gravity feels remorse, but to do anything more would mean bringing its final hug to an end. It is so in love with its own expression of affection that a little pain, suffering, and destruction is not enough to make it relinquish its embrace.

The rocks and boulders and things are still quite quiet. They have a different conception of time from you and I and live in perpetual fear that Gravity will suddenly stop its embrace and go back to the way it had been behaving before it realized that it was causing so much stress. The rocks wait for Gravity to forget the vow it so desperately wants to remember forever.

# How Duck Lost Her Voice

*Ken MacGregor*

Ginny pitched another piece of bread in the water. The ducks jostled for position to get it. The ducks who lost the race were very vocal in their disappointment.

"Dada," Ginny said, tugging on her father's shirt with thumb and forefinger, "why do ducks quack like that?"

Ginny's father hunkered down next to his daughter and looked out across the pond. Their heads were only inches apart. Turning toward Ginny, he kissed her on the cheek. Immediately, she wiped it off. Ginny had no interest in kisses.

"Well, honey, all ducks are very resentful and that's the noise they make to let us know."

"What's 'resentful?'"

"It means angry about something someone else did, kind of like 'bitter.' You know that one?" Ginny shook her head. "Grumpy?" Ginny nodded. "Okay. Ducks are resentful because of something that happened a long time ago when the world was still new and animals could talk."

"Animals used to talk?"

"Oh yes. Some more than others, of course.

Sloth, for example would only toss out a word every few minutes, so anyone wanting to have a conversation with Sloth would have to be very patient. Bird and Monkey, however, were two animals who chattered constantly. By themselves they were noisy enough, but when they got together, their voices came out all at once, so it sounded like a single, incredibly loud sound."

"And ducks talked, too, didn't they?" Ginny asked. Her eyes shone, her interest piqued.

"They did," her father said. "They spoke very well, in fact."

Ginny followed her father to the bench. She waited until he sat down and climbed up on his lap. He brushed an errant strand of hair behind his daughter's ear.

Ginny gave her father a smile filled with love.

"So: once, when the world was new the animals could all talk. Nowadays, animals don't talk, except for certain birds who can imitate speech. Oh, but back then, all species could talk to one another. It made for much greater understanding than we have now."

"Dada, did Tiger talk to Rabbit?"

"Well, yes, honey, she did, but Rabbit didn't much like what Tiger had to say."

"Why not?" Ginny asked.

"Well, honey, tigers are carnivores. They eat rabbits."

"That's terrible," Ginny said.

"Well, it's terrible for rabbits."

Ginny scrunched her eyebrows together. She tilted her head to one side. Her father kept quiet and waited.

"But," Ginny said, "it's not so bad for tigers, right?"

Her father grinned. He put his hand up for a high-five and Ginny slapped it with her own.

"Now, Duck was very fond of her own voice. To be fair, her voice was indeed lovely. When Duck spoke kindly, the other animals were enchanted. She could read a grocery list and it would sound like poetry. Some folks who have beautiful voices have beautiful hearts to go with them. Unfortunately, Duck wasn't like that. She hardly ever spoke kindly. Duck was just plain mean."

Ginny leaned her head on her father's chest and felt the rumble of his voice as he continued his tale.

"Walking along the wide river that sparkled in the sun, Duck saw Snake sunning himself on a rock. 'Where are your legs?' she asked him.

"'Don't have legs,' said Snake.

"'Lame,' said Duck. 'How do you get anywhere?' she asked.

"'I slither,' Snake said. He showed Duck what he meant by slithering along the ground for a few feet.

"'That's weird and creepy, and I don't like it,' said Duck. She poked snake with her sharp beak, hurting him. Snake slithered away, heading north as fast as he could. 'Legs are so much better," Duck said to herself, holding up one webbed foot, then the other to admire them.

"Further along, Duck came across Chipmunk, who was busy stuffing acorns into her cheeks to eat later. 'Your face is grotesquely fat,' said Duck. 'Look at my face: it is narrow and smooth and handsome.'

"Chipmunk tried to explain that it was acorns making her cheeks bulge, but her mouth was so full, Duck couldn't understand her words.

"'Not only do you have a fat face,' Duck went on, 'but you mumble. You are rude and unpleasant.'

"Chipmunk tried to say *look who's talking*, but it came out all garbled. Duck went on.

"'You should try to be more like me. I am quite nice to look at and I have a fine voice.' Duck bent down and pecked Chipmunk painfully with her beak.

"A surprisingly clear 'ow!' came from Chipmunk's mouth, along with a whole acorn. But, Duck was already walking away and didn't see. Chipmunk ran to the north as fast as she could.

"After a while, Duck left the river to stroll along the forest path. It was a lovely, warm day and a layer of leaves on the ground rustled softly beneath her feet. Enough sun came through the canopy of trees to warm the feathers on Duck's back. She shook them, preening a bit. From behind a tree, a long, low shape slid onto the path. The shape had a squarish head with pointy ears and eyes that caught the light and reflected it like polished stones.

"'What sort of creature are you?' Duck asked.

"'I am a jaguar,' said Jaguar. 'You have a lovely voice, Duck. Do you sing?'

"Duck sniffed in a very haughty sort of way. 'Certainly not,' she said. 'Singing is for silly little fools.'

"'Oh, I don't know,' said Jaguar. 'I sometimes sing. Usually, after a good meal.'

"'Oh? What do you eat?' asked Duck.

"A big smile stretched across Jaguar's face. It was an unpleasant kind of smile, and Duck didn't like the look of it at all. Several very sharp teeth were revealed in that smile. Duck shivered.

"'I eat small animals and birds,' said Jaguar.

"'B-birds?' said Duck. Jaguar nodded.

"'That's horrible,' said Duck. Jaguar shrugged.

"'Maybe for the birds,' he said. 'Besides, don't you eat bugs and crayfish?'

"'Yes,' said Duck, 'but that's hardly the same thing. You're a beast.'

"Jaguar leaned closer to Duck and licked his still-smiling lips. 'A very hungry beast.'

"Quick as a blink, Duck pecked Jaguar right between his eyes. Jaguar squeezed his eyes shut in sudden pain. While Jaguar's eyes were closed, Duck spread her wings and leaped into the air. Duck could fly for short distances, but she preferred to walk."

"Jaguar is kinda scary," Ginny said. She had shivered a little, too, like Duck.

"To a duck, certainly," her father said.

"To me, too."

She turned to him, wrapping both arms around his neck and hugged him tightly. After several seconds, she looked up into his eyes.

"What happened next?" Ginny asked. "After Duck landed, I mean."

"Well, she flew far enough that she was out of the trees, so if Jaguar was angry or hungry enough to chase her, Duck would see him coming. Duck landed in the low grass of the plains. At one time, the grass had been much higher, but many animals came and ate it. Now, the grass only came to Duck's belly, which was only a few inches off the ground. It tickled her under-feathers a bit as she walked, heading generally north, which was where the big animals lived. After her encounter with Jaguar, Duck wanted to be closer to animals who could protect her. Anyone would think twice before starting trouble with Rhinoceros or Hippopotamus. Several times, Duck checked behind her to make sure Jaguar wasn't coming from the trees, but she didn't see him, so she relaxed. In the distance, Duck could see a group of animals gathered. Curious, she waddled in their direction. Elephant was there, and she was listening to the other animals tell her something. Elephant was kind of like a judge or a police officer for the animals. She was wise and fair, and very large, so everyone listened to her."

Ginny giggled. Her father paused and looked at her.

"It's just funny. Elephant police. I picture an elephant in a blue uniform with a hat and a badge."

Her father smiled.

"Yep. That's funny all right."

"Tell the story," Ginny said.

"As Duck approached the group of animals, she saw who the others were. In a rough circle with Elephant stood Snake, Chipmunk and Jaguar. Duck stopped when she saw who it was. Elephant noticed Duck first, but soon the others saw her, too. For a long moment, the animals stared at Duck and she stared back and nobody said anything. Finally, Elephant cleared her throat.

"'Duck, these three say you have been very mean to them and that you pecked each of them with your sharp beak.' Duck was flustered. She shook out her feathers and blinked several times.

"'Oh, Elephant,' Duck said, 'I wasn't at all mean to these other animals. I merely pointed out their faults so they could better themselves. When I did, they became belligerent and that's when I pecked them. And, in the case of Jaguar who basically threatened to eat me, it was self-defense.'

"At this point, Elephant looked at Jaguar, who shrugged. 'I'm a carnivore,' he said. 'I was just being honest.'

"Elephant considered his words, and the explanation Duck gave. She deliberated for quite some time, while the animals waited around her. Jaguar's stomach growled and the other animals slowly moved around behind Elephant's legs. Jaguar made a face, but stayed where he was."

"Everyone is afraid of Jaguar," Ginny said.

"Not Elephant," her father said.

"No. Because Elephant is so big. That's why she's in charge, right?"

Her father nodded and smiled.

"Finally," he continued, "Elephant looked down at Duck, hiding behind Elephant's foreleg. With her trunk, Elephant pulled Duck out into the open and set her on the ground. Duck trembled visibly as she awaited Elephant's judgment. Jaguar licked his lips and Duck gulped loudly.

"'Do you see that I am in the right?' Duck asked.

"Elephant gave Duck a long look and shook her head. 'It seems to me, Duck, that you have a very high opinion of yourself and a very low opinion of everyone else,' Elephant said.

"'Well, that's just your opinion,' Duck said.

"The other three animals spoke up. They argued, that no, Elephant was pretty much right.

"'Well, what do you know anyway,' Duck asked. She was angry and embarrassed and lashed out, pecking Elephant on the foot. It was the only part of Elephant she could reach. Duck pecked that foot with all her might, again and again. Until it actually started to hurt Elephant's foot, just a little.

"Glaring down at Duck, Elephant stepped on

Duck's sharp beak. Under the immense weight of Elephant's foot, Duck's sharp beak was squashed and flattened. When Elephant raised her leg again, Duck pulled away with a loud and indignant *quack*. She looked stunned at the noise that had come from her flattened beak, which was now a bill. Duck's beautiful voice was replaced by a silly-sounding honking noise.

"'Quack?' she asked, but the elephant gave no answer. Jaguar, who didn't particularly care what his dinner sounded like, inched toward Duck, who flapped her wings and flew away. She flew as far as she could, until she grew too tired and had to land. Duck came down in the middle of a quiet pond. She sat on the water and cried. Her lovely voice was gone, flattened, along with her beak, into a goofy quack. Duck was embarrassed and for a long time wouldn't let anyone see her.

"But, eventually, she got used to the way she was now. She could still catch worms, grubs and crayfish with her new bill so she ate well. And, whenever Duck had anything mean to say, it always came out as *quack*. After a while, Duck stopped criticizing the other animals. She was much happier for it, and spent most of her time swimming and flying. Ever since, all ducks have squashed flat bills and funny voices."

"So, if you're mean to everyone, an elephant will step on your face?"

"Not really. At least, I don't think so. Better not to find out, maybe."

Ginny and her father walked away from the pond. The ducks watched them go.

# How the Elephant Fell

*Liam Hogan*

The mighty Elephant thundered along the jungle path, the tall trees shaking in his wake. "Oooh!" panted the Monkey, swinging through the branches beside him. "Where do *you* go in such a hurry?"

The Elephant cast him a contemptuous glance and slowed his pace a fraction. "I go to the woods, beneath the falls, below the mountain of the moon," he trumpeted. "There to eat my fill of the delicious fruit that hangs from the trees."

The Monkey scratched his head, puzzled. "And how will you cross the river, so high up? Surely you should descend to the plains and cross at the ford by the ancient—"

"Too long!" interrupted the Elephant. "I cross by the fallen tree over the ravine just after the falls."

The Monkey chortled. He knew the fallen tree the Elephant spoke of—all the beasts of the jungle did. "Oh Elephant! I'm afraid your journey is a wasted one and you'll have to take the long way round after all. That bridge will not take your weight!"

"Monkey," said Elephant, coldly. "Are you

aware that the muscles in my trunk are immensely strong and that I am more than capable of crushing the life out of an insignificant creature such as yourself?"

The Monkey paused, pondering this strange question. "Well, yes. But I don't see how that changes anything—the bridge is still too weak..."

Quick as a flash, the trunk darted out and seized the Monkey around his waist. Lifting the Monkey aloft, the Elephant dangled him before his eyes.

"You think I'm a fool, Monkey? I know you, I know your kind; you like the fruit of those trees just as much as I do. Is it a coincidence that today of all days you cross my path, that your lies try to slow me down? I think not! Monkey, I am wise to your deceit. You hope to strip the trees bare before I even arrive! Now admit it, the bridge *is* strong enough for me, am I right?"

The Monkey squirmed. "Well, I'm sorry to be the bearer of bad news, but no..."

The trunk squeezed.

"Arghh! Yes! Yes! You're right! You're always right!" gasped the Monkey. "Please, mighty Elephant! Let me go!"

The Elephant gave one last squeeze before he tossed the Monkey behind him and thundered on down the path.

The Monkey gingerly picked himself up, dusted himself down, and looked disdainfully after the Elephant. He'd only been trying to help. Every year, the fallen tree trunk got a little weaker, worn away by the elements and hollowed out by the insects. Why, this year, there were even nests of wasps hanging beneath it, chewing the wood to make their paper homes. He decided to follow the Elephant and see what would happen next.

The Elephant thundered on along the jungle path, 'til he was suddenly aware that there was something making almost as much noise as he was, a short way ahead. He slowed as he entered the clearing.

"What-ho, Elephant!" cried the Boar joyously, chewing on a root. "Long time no see! What brings you to these parts?"

The Elephant narrowed his eyes. There was always something...disrespectful...about the Boar's demeanour. "I go to the woods, beneath the falls, below the mountain of the moon!" he trumpeted. "There to eat my fill of the delicious fruit that hangs from the trees."

The Boar looked at the Elephant, and then the path he was taking, and back once more to the Elephant. "Oh Elephant!" he guffawed. "You can't go this way! This way leads to the ravine and the bridge there will not take your weight. You will have to descend to the plains. Here, let me show you the way—"

"Boar," said Elephant, coldly. "Are you aware that my tusks, which are so much longer and sharper than yours, could easily pin and skewer a lowly creature such as yourself?"

The Boar scratched at his hindquarters. "Well, yes, I dare say they could. But I don't see how that changes anything—you're still too heavy for the bridge."

"Oh, *am* I?" the Elephant bellowed and in a trice he'd flipped the Boar on his side and pinned him against the buttress of an immense tree. "Evil, spiteful Boar!" spat the Elephant. "More delays, more deceit! I know you and your kind, and you too are after my fruit. You hope to devour all the fallen fruit before I even arrive! You think me such a fool? That bridge was strong enough last year, and the year before, and the year before that. It will be strong enough this year. Am I right?"

The Boar tapped one of his tusks against the white bars of his prison and gulped. "Well, Elephant, actually, no..."

The Elephant twisted his head, pinching the Boar's body between his tusks. "Am I *right*?"

"Yes! Yes, you're right!" winced the Boar.

"You're always right! Please, mighty Elephant, let me go!"

The Elephant gave one little twist more and then as the Boar squealed he let him go, and thundered on down the path.

The Boar licked at his coat where the tusks had dug in and looked after the Elephant in shock. He'd only been trying to help. It was true, the bridge had been strong enough last year, and the year before that, but every year the Elephant got heavier and heavier. Something would eventually have to give. He decided to follow the Elephant—at a safe distance—and see what happened next.

The Elephant crashed to a halt at the edge of the jungle and looked out across the ravine, catching his breath. He remembered the rich, honeyed taste of the succulent fruits as if it were yesterday and not a whole year since they had last been in season. And now that it was but a short walk down to the woods where he would be tasting them once again, he allowed his hunger and his memory to mingle together into heady, blissful thoughts of the feast to come.

"Ho there, Elephant!" a thin voice trilled.

The Elephant peered around, annoyed to have his spell broken, but could see no-one.

"Hey! Down here! In front of you!" It was the

Mouse.

The Elephant eyed him suspiciously. "Mouse," he said. "I'm in a hurry."

"Oh?" said the Mouse, cleaning a whisker. "And where is it you're going to?"

"I go to the woods, beneath the falls, below the mountain of the moon," Elephant trumpeted, as his tummy rumbled. "There to eat my fill of the delicious fruit that hangs from the trees."

The Mouse looked up at him, and then over his shoulder at the ravine and the old rotten tree trunk that spanned it. "You're not...going over the bridge, are you?"

"AND WHY NOT?" The Elephant blasted, the hot air pinning the Mouse's ears back to the side of his head.

Mouse blinked. "Well, it's not safe. It won't take your weight. Please, Elephant, reconsider. Go via the ford down by the ancient—"

"Oh!" roared the Elephant. "Ahah! I see how it is. You're all in it together! So, little mouse, *you* would cross by the bridge?"

"Well, yes but..."

"And Monkey, he would cross by the bridge?"

"Indeed he would, however..."

"And Boar, he would cross by the bridge?"

"Yes, yes, but..."

"But you don't want *me* to cross by the bridge?!" the Elephant roared and the skies darkened as flocks of birds took flight from the trees overlooking the falls.

"I'm sorry, I don't really..."

"Mouse," said Elephant, coldly. "Are you aware of how big and heavy my feet are?"

"That's what I've been trying to tell you!" piped Mouse.

"Heavy enough to crush a pitiful creature such as yourself?" the Elephant continued.

"Well...yes..." said the Mouse slowly. "And heavy enough to break the bridge..."

With a harrumph, the Elephant swung one foot forward and over the Mouse's head until it blotted out the sky, lowering it until it touched the Mouse's back, who frantically tried to find a hollow to flatten himself into.

"Despicable Mouse!" roared the Elephant. "If the bridge is strong enough for the three of you, it will be strong enough for me. Am I right?"

There was a muffled squeak from beneath the Elephant's foot. "Speak up, little Mouse!" the Elephant laughed, as he eased his foot down a fraction.

"Yes! *Yes*! You are right! You're always right!" shrieked Mouse at the top of his voice. "Oh, mighty, magnificent Elephant, the biggest and best of us all, please, raise your foot and let a pitiful, lowly, insignificant creature live!"

The Elephant smiled and slowly lifted his foot. "There," he said. "That wasn't so very hard, was it?" And he sauntered over to the fallen log.

He eyed it cautiously. He was quite, *quite* sure it would take his weight—it always had, hadn't it? And yet, the warnings of the other animals had cast their seed of doubt. What if it didn't? It was an awfully long way down. Perhaps it would be more prudent...

He turned around, took one step back along the path he had come and then saw, on the brow of the little hill above him, the Monkey, the Boar, and the Mouse watching him attentively. He raised his trunk, gave them a cheery wave, screwed up his courage, turned and carefully stepped out onto the bridge.

When he had passed into the woods beyond, the Monkey turned to the other two. "What do we do now?"

The Mouse sat down, rubbing his still tender head. "We wait," he said, grimly.

The Elephant was gone a very long time. The ripe fruit was indeed plentiful and good and with his long trunk he could strip it from the lower branches, as well as pick it up from the ground where it fell. When he returned to the bridge over the ravine, he'd almost forgotten the warnings and his own short-lived fear, until, when he was about half-way across, the old tree trunk gave an ominous groan and a cloud of angry wasps took flight. He froze in mid-stride.

"Oh Elephant!" He heard his name called out and looked up in surprise to see the Monkey, the Boar, and the Mouse waiting by the end of the bridge. "How was the fruit?"

"Delicious," he replied, nervously, quietly.

"Did you eat your fill?" asked Mouse. "I'm sure you did! Tell me, how much heavier do you think you are now, than when earlier you crossed this termite-infested log?"

"I...er..." the Elephant faltered as he heard something crack and looked over the side to see a large chunk of rotten wood spinning into the abyss below.

"And yet you were right!" laughed the Mouse. "The bridge *did* take your weight. Oh mighty beast, you're always right! Even though the wood is more rotten than ever before, and you, you are heavier than ever before, I'm sure it could also take the weight of Boar here..."

The Boar hopped up onto the log, his heavy feet

sending tremors down its length to where the Elephant stood, still frozen in fear.

"... and Monkey..."

Monkey swung up onto the trunk and whooped in excitement, causing the bridge to sway gently back and forth.

"... *and* little old me!" said the Mouse, as he scampered up to stand between the Boar and the Monkey.

There was silence for a moment. The whole jungle seemed to hold its breath as the trunk creaked and groaned. One heartbeat. Two. Three. The Elephant opened his half-closed eyes.

"See?" he said triumphantly. "I was..."

But the "RIGHT" was a scream, as with an almighty crack the aged tree trunk split in two. The Monkey, the Boar and the Mouse all jumped clear, but the Elephant was stranded in the middle of the log and could do nothing but follow the rotten wood down into the ravine.

And that, dearly beloved, is how the mighty Elephant fell.

# Why the Sea is Salt

*Edward Ahern*

*This is a retelling of and homage to "Why the Sea is Salt," a story included by Sir George Webbe Dasent in his 1904 book,* Popular Tales From the Norse. *The language is modern but the spirit is hopefully as it was once told.*

Once, a long, long time ago, there were two brothers. One was rich and mean and the other poor and good hearted. The morning of one Christmas Eve the poor brother had not a shred of meat or crumb of bread. He went to his rich brother's house to beg for enough food to make a meal for him and his wife on Christmas day.

The mean spirited brother wasn't glad to see his face nor willing to help him, but in the end he said, "If you do as I ask you, I'll give you a whole side of bacon."

"I'll do anything for you, brother. Thank you so much and Merry Christmas."

"Well, here is the side of bacon. Now go straight to hell."

"I've given my word so I must stick to it," said the poor brother. He threw the side of bacon over his shoulder and set off. He walked all day, not knowing where he was going. At dusk he saw the light of a fire and turned off into the woods. "Maybe this is the place."

He came out of the woods to a dark house and saw an old, old man with a long white beard who was chopping wood for the Christmas fire.

"Good even," said the poor man.

"The same to you. Where are you going so late on Christmas Eve?"

"Ah. I need to go to hell, but I don't know the way."

The old man smiled. "Well, you're not far off, for this is the entrance to Hell. It's easy to get in, not so easy to get out, but you seem a good man and should have no problem. Meat is scarce in hell, and once you get inside the imps will be begging you to sell your bacon. But don't sell it unless they give you the stone quern sitting just inside the door. When you come out with it I'll teach you how to use it. If you use the quern properly it will grind out almost anything."

The poor man said thank you very politely, walked over, and knocked loudly on the devil's door.

Once inside the door the poor man found things just as he'd been told. The imps swarmed over him like ants, each trying to outbid the other for the side of bacon.

"Well," he said, "rightfully my wife and I should have this bacon for our Christmas dinner, but if I sell it at all I will only exchange it for the quern hidden behind the door."

The devil himself walked up. He chaffered and haggled with the poor man, but the devil wanted that side of bacon so badly that at last he agreed to give up his quern.

Once back outside the devil's door the poor man asked the old woodcutter how to use the quern. And the snowy bearded woodcutter showed him all the secret little ways in which the quern must be used. He thanked the woodcutter and marched back home carrying the heavy stone quern, but it was Christmas Eve midnight before he reached his own house.

"Wherever in the world have you been?" asked his dame. "Here I've sat hour after hour without so much as two sticks to fire up, nor the Christmas porridge to be heated."

"Ah," said the man. "I just couldn't get back before. For one thing I had a long way to go and for another I had a long way to come back. But now you'll see what you'll see."

He heaved the quern onto the table, and ordered

it to grind out lighted candles, and table cloth, and meat, and ale, and so on, until they had everything nice for a Christmas meal. His dame stood by blessing herself and asking him where he'd gotten such a wonderful quern, but of course he didn't tell her.

"It's all one where I got it," he said, "but the quern is a marvel and the mill stream never freezes, and that's good enough for us."

He ground out meat and drink and dainties enough to last 'til Twelfth Day. On the third day of Christmas he invited all his friends and family to his cottage and provided them a great feast. But when his rich, mean brother saw all that was laid out on the table and set aside in the larder, he boiled up spiteful and wild, for he couldn't abide that his brother had such things.

"It was only Christmas Eve," he told those attending, "he was in such trouble that he came to me and begged in God's name for a morsel of food. Now he gives us a feast as if he were count or king."

He turned to his poor brother and asked, "From where, in Hell's name, did you get all these wonderful things?"

"Oh, from just behind the door," he replied, and would say no more. But later in the evening, after he had drunk many mugs of ale, he relented. "This is how we now have everything we need," he said, and took the quern from out of a cabinet. He gathered the guests and ordered the quern to produce fine flaxen cloth, and good ale, and several pairs of boots in his size.

When the rich brother saw this he swore he must have the quern, and set about with twisted words to convince his brother to part with it. "You've so much now, you've no need for more," he said. "But I do. Just let me keep the quern till hay harvest is over, and I'll give you three hundred pieces of silver."

For the rich brother thought to force the quern to spew out meat and drink and cloth to last for years. It would grow no moss while in his possession. And the poor brother, in sympathy, agreed. But he didn't quite trust his brother, and taught him only part of what was needed to control the quern.

The rich brother carried the quern home that evening, and the next morning told his wife to go out into the field and toss the grass while the mowers cut it. "I'll stay at home and get dinner ready."

When the time for dinner came near the rich brother set the quern on his kitchen table and said, "Grind herrings and broth, and grind them faster and faster."

And the quern began to furiously grind herrings and broth. The rich man filled all the dishes, then all the pots and tubs, but the quern churned faster and faster, spewing herrings and broth all over the kitchen floor.

He twisted the quern, and twirled it and yelled at it, but for all his twisting and twirling the quern just ground the faster. The rich man threw open the kitchen door and ran into his parlor, but the herring broth gushed behind him, and almost drowned him before he could throw open his house door and run down the path.

As he ran the herring and broth washed in waves behind him, roaring like a waterfall over the farm. His old dame, who was still in the field tossing hay, thought it was past time for dinner and called to the field hands.

"Even though the master hasn't called us in we may as well go. It may be he finds it hard work to boil the broth and will be glad of my help."

The men were glad, and they all were walking slowly back towards the farmhouse when the master came running and screaming toward them, chased by billowing waves of herrings and broth. As he ran by the rich man yelled, "If only you each had a hundred throats! Take care that you're not drowned in broth."

And the rich man ran on, as if the devil himself were behind him, all the way to the poor man's house. "Please, for God's sake," he cried to his brother, "take back the quern. If it grinds an hour more the whole parish will be buried in herrings and broth."

"All right," said the poor brother, "but you'll have to pay me another three hundred silver pieces."

So the poor brother got back the quern as well as more silver. He built a big farmhouse along the sea shore, and plated it all over with gold. On a sunny day the golden house gleamed and glistened far out over the sea. All who sailed by put ashore to get a closer look at the golden house and the rich man who owned the magic quern—for he was the poor brother no more, now far richer than his brother had ever been.

The fame of the gold house and the rich man's quern spread far and wide, 'til there was no one who hadn't heard of it. One day a ship's captain came and asked the brother to see the quern. "Such a little thing," he marveled. "Can it grind salt?"

"Grind salt!" said the brother. "Of course it can. It can churn out anything."

"Ah," said the captain. "For years and years I've

risked voyages across stormy seas to bring ship loads of salt back to my home. Please, at almost any cost, sell me the quern so I can safely do my business."

The brother said he couldn't bear to part with his quern, but the captain begged and prayed and asked and pleaded. And at last the brother thought to himself that he was rich enough for several lifetimes and the quern could be put to good use.

"Very well," he said."Give me a thousand pieces of silver and the quern shall be yours."

The captain was excited to get the quern, but afraid that the brother would change his mind, so he paid the brother and rushed back to his ship without asking how to stop the quern from churning.

Once he'd sailed a few miles from shore the captain hauled the quern out on deck and said, "Grind salt, and grind it good and fast."

The quern ground salt so fast that it flowed out like sand in the desert. The salt poured into the ship's holds, and into its cabins and piled in mountains on the deck. The captain desperately tried to stop the quern's churning, but no matter what he said or how he handled it, the quern kept spewing salt. And finally the heap of salt grew so high that the ship sank, and the quern with it.

And there the quern sits to this day, at the bottom of the sea, grinding away. And that's why the sea is salt.

# How the First Letter Was Written

*Rudyard Kipling*

Once upon a most early time was a Neolithic man.
He was not a Jute or an Angle, or even a
Dravidian, which he might well have been, Best
Beloved, but never mind why. He was a Primitive,
and he lived cavily in a Cave, and he wore very
few clothes, and he couldn't read and he couldn't
write and he didn't want to, and except when he
was hungry he was quite happy. His name was
Tegumai Bopsulai, and that means, "Man-who-
does-not-put-his-foot-forward-in-a-hurry"; but we,
O Best Beloved, will call him Tegumai, for short.
And his wife's name was Teshumai Tewindrow,
and that means, "Lady-who-asks-a-very-many-
questions"; but we, O Best Beloved, will call her
Teshumai, for short. And his little girl-daughter's
name was Taffimai Metallumai, and that means,
"Small-person-without-any-manners-who-ought-
to-be-spanked"; but I'm going to call her Taffy.
And she was Tegumai Bopsulai's Best Beloved
and her own Mummy's Best Beloved, and she was
not spanked half as much as was good for her; and
they were all three very happy. As soon as Taffy
could run about she went everywhere with her

Daddy Tegumai, and sometimes they would not come home to the Cave till they were hungry, and then Teshumai Tewindrow would say, "Where in the world have you two been to, to get so shocking dirty? Really, my Tegumai, you're no better than my Taffy."

Now attend and listen!

One day Tegumai Bopsulai went down through the beaver-swamp to the Wagai river to spear carp-fish for dinner, and Taffy went too. Tegumai's spear was made of wood with shark's teeth at the end, and before he had caught any fish at all he accidentally broke it clean across by jabbing it down too hard on the bottom of the river. They were miles and miles from home (of course they had their lunch with them in a little bag), and Tegumai had forgotten to bring any extra spears.

"Here's a pretty kettle of fish!" said Tegumai. "It will take me half the day to mend this."

"There's your big black spear at home," said Taffy. "Let me run back to the Cave and ask Mummy to give it me."

"It's too far for your little fat legs," said Tegumai. "Besides, you might fall into the beaver-swamp and be drowned. We must make the best of a bad job." He sat down and took out a little leather mendy-bag, full of reindeer-sinews and strips of leather, and lumps of bee's-wax and resin, and began to mend the spear.

Taffy sat down too, with her toes in the water and her chin in her hand, and thought very hard. Then she said—"I say, Daddy, it's an awful nuisance that you and I don't know how to write, isn't it? If we did we could send a message for the new spear."

"Taffy," said Tegumai, "how often have I told you not to use slang? 'Awful' isn't a pretty word, but it could be a convenience, now you mention it, if we could write home."

Just then a Stranger-man came along the river, but he belonged to a far tribe, the Tewaras, and he did not understand one word of Tegumai's language. He stood on the bank and smiled at Taffy, because he had a little girl-daughter of his own at home. Tegumai drew a hank of deer-sinews from his mendy-bag and began to mend his spear.

"Come here," said Taffy. "Do you know where my Mummy lives?" And the Stranger-man said "Um!" being, as you know, a Tewara.

"Silly!" said Taffy, and she stamped her foot, because she saw a shoal of very big carp going up the river just when her Daddy couldn't use his spear.

"Don't bother grown-ups," said Tegumai, so

busy with his spear-mending that he did not turn round.

"I aren't," said Taffy. "I only want him to do what I want him to do, and he won't understand."

"Then don't bother me," said Tegumai, and he went on pulling and straining at the deer-sinews with his mouth full of loose ends. The Stranger-man—a genuine Tewara he was—sat down on the grass, and Taffy showed him what her Daddy was doing. The Stranger-man thought, "this is a very wonderful child. She stamps her foot at me and she makes faces. She must be the daughter of that noble Chief who is so great that he won't take any notice of me." So he smiled more politely than ever.

"Now," said Taffy, "I want you to go to my Mummy, because your legs are longer than mine, and you won't fall into the beaver-swamp, and ask for Daddy's other spear—the one with the black handle that hangs over our fireplace."

The Stranger-man (and he was a Tewara) thought, "This is a very, very wonderful child. She waves her arms and she shouts at me, but I don't understand a word of what she says. But if I don't do what she wants, I greatly fear that that haughty Chief, Man-who-turns-his-back-on-callers, will be angry." He got up and twisted a big flat piece of bark off a birch-tree and gave it to Taffy. He did this, Best Beloved, to show that his heart was as white as the birch-bark and that he meant no harm; but Taffy didn't quite understand.

"Oh!" said she. "Now I see! You want my Mummy's living-address? Of course I can't write, but I can draw pictures if I've anything sharp to scratch with. Please lend me the shark's tooth off your necklace."

The Stranger-man (and he was a Tewara) didn't say anything, So Taffy put up her little hand and pulled at the beautiful bead and seed and shark-tooth necklace round his neck.

The Stranger-man (and he was a Tewara) thought, "This is a very, very, very wonderful child. The shark's tooth on my necklace is a magic shark's tooth, and I was always told that if anybody touched it without my leave they would immediately swell up or burst, but this child doesn't swell up or burst, and that important Chief, Man-who-attends-strictly-to-his-business, who has not yet taken any notice of me at all, doesn't seem to be afraid that she will swell up or burst. I had better be more polite."

So he gave Taffy the shark's tooth, and she lay down flat on her tummy with her legs in the air, like some people on the drawing-room floor when they want to draw pictures, and she said, "Now I'll draw you some beautiful pictures! You can look over my shoulder, but you mustn't joggle. First I'll draw Daddy fishing. It isn't very like him; but Mummy will know, because I've drawn his spear all broken. Well, now I'll draw the other spear that he wants, the black-handled spear. It looks as if it was sticking in Daddy's back, but that's because the shark's tooth slipped and this piece of bark isn't big enough. That's the spear I want you to fetch; so I'll draw a picture of me myself 'splaining to you. My hair doesn't stand up like I've drawn, but it's easier to draw that way. Now I'll draw you. I think you're very nice really, but I can't make you pretty in the picture, so you mustn't be 'fended. Are you 'fended?"

The Stranger-man (and he was a Tewara) smiled. He thought, "There must be a big battle going to be fought somewhere, and this extraordinary child, who takes my magic shark's tooth but who does not swell up or burst, is telling me to call all the great Chief's tribe to help him. He is a great Chief, or he would have noticed me."

"Look," said Taffy, drawing very hard and rather scratchily, "now I've drawn you, and I've put the spear that Daddy wants into your hand, just to remind you that you're to bring it. Now I'll show you how to find my Mummy's living-address. You go along till you come to two trees (those are trees), and then you go over a hill (that's a hill), and then you come into a beaver-swamp all full of beavers. I haven't put in all the beavers, because I can't draw beavers, but I've drawn their heads, and that's all you'll see of them when you cross the swamp. Mind you don't fall in! Then our Cave is just beyond the beaver-swamp. It isn't as high as the hills really, but I can't draw things very small. That's my Mummy outside. She is beautiful. She is the most beautifullest Mummy there ever was, but she won't be 'fended when she sees I've drawn her so plain. She'll be pleased of me because I can draw. Now, in case you forget, I've drawn the spear that Daddy wants outside our Cave. It's inside really, but you show the picture to my Mummy and she'll give it you. I've made her holding up her hands, because I know she'll be so pleased to see you. Isn't it a beautiful picture? And do you quite understand, or shall I 'splain again?"

The Stranger-man (and he was a Tewara) looked at the picture and nodded very hard. He said to himself, "If I do not fetch this great Chief's tribe to help him, he will be slain by his enemies who are coming up on all sides with spears. Now I see why the great Chief pretended not to notice me! He feared that his enemies were hiding in the bushes and would see him. Therefore he turned to me his back, and let the wise and wonderful child draw the terrible picture showing me his difficulties. I will away and get help for him from his tribe." He did not even ask Taffy the road, but raced off into the bushes like the wind, with the birch-bark in his hand, and Taffy sat down most pleased.

Now this is the picture that Taffy had drawn for him!

"What have you been doing, Taffy?" said Tegumai. He had mended his spear and was carefully waving it to and fro.

"It's a little berangement of my own, Daddy dear," said Taffy. "If you won't ask me questions, you'll know all about it in a little time, and you'll be surprised. You don't know how surprised you'll be, Daddy! Promise you'll be surprised."

"Very well," said Tegumai, and went on fishing.

The Stranger-man—did you know he was a Tewara?—hurried away with the picture and ran for some miles, till quite by accident he found Teshumai Tewindrow at the door of her Cave, talking to some other Neolithic ladies who had come in to a Primitive lunch. Taffy was very like Teshumai, especially about the upper part of the face and the eyes, so the Stranger-man—always a pure Tewara—smiled politely and handed Teshumai the birch-bark. He had run hard, so that he panted, and his legs were scratched with brambles, but he still tried to be polite.

As soon as Teshumai saw the picture she screamed like anything and flew at the Stranger-man. The other Neolithic ladies at once knocked him down and sat on him in a long line of six, while Teshumai pulled his hair.

"It's as plain as the nose on this Stranger-man's face," she said. "He has stuck my Tegumai all full of spears, and frightened poor Taffy so that her hair stands all on end; and not content with that, he brings me a horrid picture of how it was done. Look!" She showed the picture to all the Neolithic ladies sitting patiently on the Stranger-man. "Here is my Tegumai with his arm broken; here is a spear sticking into his back; here is a man with a spear ready to throw; here is another man throwing a spear from a Cave, and here are a whole pack of people" (they were Taffy's beavers really, but they did look rather like people) "coming up behind Tegumai. Isn't it shocking!"

"Most shocking!" said the Neolithic ladies, and they filled the Stranger-man's hair with mud (at which he was surprised), and they beat upon the Reverberating Tribal Drums, and called together all the chiefs of the Tribe of Tegumai, with their Hetmans and Dolmans, all Neguses, Woons, and Akhoonds of the organisation, in addition to the Warlocks, Angekoks, Juju-men, Bonzes, and the rest, who decided that before they chopped the Stranger-man's head off he should instantly lead them down to the river and show them where he had hidden poor Taffy.

By this time the Stranger-man (in spite of being a Tewara) was really annoyed. They had filled his hair quite solid with mud; they had rolled him up and down on knobby pebbles; they had sat upon him in a long line of six; they had thumped him and bumped him till he could hardly breathe; and though he did not understand their language, he was almost sure that the names the Neolithic ladies called him were not ladylike. However, he said nothing till all the Tribe of Tegumai were assembled, and then he led them back to the bank of the Wagai river, and there they found Taffy making daisy-chains, and Tegumai carefully spearing small carp with his mended spear.

"Well, you have been quick!" said Taffy. "But why did you bring so many people? Daddy dear, this is my surprise. Are you surprised, Daddy?"

"Very," said Tegumai; "but it has ruined all my fishing for the day. Why, the whole dear, kind, nice, clean, quiet Tribe is here, Taffy."

And so they were. First of all walked Teshumai Tewindrow and the Neolithic ladies, tightly holding on to the Stranger-man, whose hair was full of mud (although he was a Tewara). Behind them came the Head Chief, the Vice-Chief, the Deputy and Assistant Chiefs (all armed to the upper teeth), the Hetmans and Heads of Hundreds, Platoffs with their Platoons, and Dolmans with their Detachments; Woons, Neguses, and Akhoonds ranking in the rear (still armed to the teeth). Behind them was the Tribe in hierarchical order, from owners of four caves (one for each season), a private reindeer-run, and two salmon-leaps, to feudal and prognathous Villeins, semi-entitled to half a bearskin of winter nights, seven yards from the fire, and adscript serfs, holding the reversion of a scraped marrow-bone under heriot (Aren't those beautiful words, Best Beloved?). They were all there, prancing and shouting, and they frightened every fish for twenty miles, and Tegumai thanked them in a fluid Neolithic oration.

Then Teshumai Tewindrow ran down and kissed and hugged Taffy very much indeed; but the Head Chief of the Tribe of Tegumai took Tegumai by the top-knot feathers and shook him severely.

"Explain! Explain! Explain!" cried all the Tribe of Tegumai.

"Goodness' sakes alive!" said Tegumai. "Let go

of my top-knot. Can't a man break his carp-spear without the whole countryside descending on him? You're a very interfering people."

"I don't believe you've brought my Daddy's black-handled spear after all," said Taffy. "And what are you doing to my nice Stranger-man?"

They were thumping him by twos and threes and tens till his eyes turned round and round. He could only gasp and point at Taffy.

"Where are the bad people who speared you, my darling?" said Teshumai Tewindrow.

"There weren't any," said Tegumai. "My only visitor this morning was the poor fellow that you are trying to choke. Aren't you well, or are you ill, O Tribe of Tegumai?"

"He came with a horrible picture," said the Head Chief—"a picture that showed you were full of spears."

"Er-um-Pr'aps I'd better 'splain that I gave him that picture," said Taffy, but she did not feel quite comfy.

"You!" said the Tribe of Tegumai all together. "Small-person-with-no-manners-who-ought-to-be-spanked! You?"

"Taffy dear, I'm afraid we're in for a little trouble," said her Daddy, and put his arm round her, so she didn't care.

"Explain! Explain! Explain!" said the Head Chief of the Tribe of Tegumai, and he hopped on one foot.

"I wanted the Stranger-man to fetch Daddy's

spear, so I drawded it," said Taffy. "There wasn't lots of spears. There was only one spear. I drawded it three times to make sure. I couldn't help it looking as if it stuck into Daddy's head—there wasn't room on the birch-bark; and those things that Mummy called bad people are my beavers. I drawded them to show him the way through the swamp; and I drawded Mummy at the mouth of the Cave looking pleased because he is a nice Stranger-man, and I think you are just the stupidest people in the world," said Taffy. "He is a very nice man. Why have you filled his hair with mud? Wash him!"

Nobody said anything at all for a longtime, till the Head Chief laughed; then the Stranger-man (who was at least a Tewara) laughed; then Tegumai laughed till he fell down flat on the bank; then all the Tribe laughed more and worse and louder. The only people who did not laugh were Teshumai Tewindrow and all the Neolithic ladies. They were very polite to all their husbands, and said "Idiot!" ever so often.

Then the Head Chief of the Tribe of Tegumai cried and said and sang, "O Small-person-without-any-manners-who-ought-to-be-spanked, you've hit upon a great invention!"

"I didn't intend to; I only wanted Daddy's black-handled spear," said Taffy.

"Never mind. It is a great invention, and some day men will call it writing. At present it is only pictures, and, as we have seen to-day, pictures are not always properly understood. But a time will come, O Babe of Tegumai, when we shall make letters—all twenty-six of 'em—and when we shall be able to read as well as to write, and then we shall always say exactly what we mean without any mistakes. Let the Neolithic ladies wash the mud out of the stranger's hair."

"I shall be glad of that," said Taffy, "because, after all, though you've brought every single other spear in the Tribe of Tegumai, you've forgotten my Daddy's black-handled spear."

Then the Head Chief cried and said and sang, "Taffy dear, the next time you write a picture-letter, you'd better send a man who can talk our language with it, to explain what it means. I don't mind it myself, because I am a Head Chief, but it's very bad for the rest of the Tribe of Tegumai, and, as you can see, it surprises the stranger."

Then they adopted the Stranger-man (a genuine Tewara of Tewar) into the Tribe of Tegumai, because he was a gentleman and did not make a fuss about the mud that the Neolithic ladies had put into his hair. But from that day to this (and I suppose it is all Taffy's fault), very few little girls have ever liked learning to read or write. Most of them prefer to draw pictures and play about with their Daddies—just like Taffy.

# The Tabu Tale

*Rudyard Kipling*

*Kipling wrote this particular story for the 1903 American edition, as an enticement to readers. By accident of history, it has been omitted from most editions of Just So Stories. It is our pleasure to present it to you.*

The most important thing about Tegumai Bopsulai and his dear daughter, Taffimai Metallumai, were the Tabus of Tegumai, which were all Bopsulai.

Listen and attend, and remember, O Best Beloved; because we know about Tabus, you and I.

When Taffimai Metallumai (but you can still call her Taffy) went out into the woods hunting with Tegumai, she never kept still. She kept very unstill. She danced among dead leaves, she did. She snapped dry branches off, she did. She slid down banks and pits, she did quarries and pits of sand, she did. She splashed through swamps and bogs, she did; and she made a horrible noise!

So all the animals that they hunted—squirrels, beavers, otters, badgers, and deer, and the rabbits—knew when Taffy and her Daddy were coming, and ran away.

Then Taffy said, "I'm awfully sorry, Daddy, dear." Then Tegumai said, "What's the use of being sorry? The squirrels have gone, and the beavers have dived, the deer have jumped, and the rabbits are deep in their buries. You ought to be beaten, O Daughter of Tegumai, and I would, too, if I didn't happen to love you." Just then he saw a squirrel kinking and prinking round the trunk of an ash-tree, and he said, "H'sh! There's our lunch, Taffy, if you'll only keep quiet."

Taffy said, "Where? Where? Show me! Show!" She said it in a raspy-gaspy whisper that would have frightened a steam-cow, and she skittered about in the bracken, being a 'citable child; and the squirrel flicked his tail and went off in large, free, loopy-legs to about the middle of Sussex before he ever stopped.

Tegumai was severely angry. He stood quite still, making up his mind whether it would be better to boil Taffy, or skin Taffy, or tattoo Taffy, or cut her hair, or send her to bed for one night without being kissed; and while he was thinking, the Head Chief of the Tribe of Tegumai came through the woods all in his eagle-feathers.

He was the Head Chief of the High and the Low and the Middle Medicine for the whole Tribe of Tegumai, and he and Taffy were rather friends.

He said to Tegumai, "What is the matter, O Chiefest of Bopsulai? You look angry."

"I am angry," said Tegumai, and he told the Head Chief all about Taffy's very unstillness in the woods; and about the way she frightened the game; and about her falling into swamps because she would look behind her when she ran; and about her falling out of trees because she wouldn't take good hold on both sides of her; and about her getting her legs all greeny with duckweed from ponds and places, and bringing it sploshing into the Cave. The Head Chief shook his head till the eagle-feathers and the little shells on his forehead rattled, and then he said, "Well, well! I'll see about it later. I wanted to talk to you, O Tegumai, on serious business."

"Talk away, O Head Chief," said Tegumai, and they both sat down politely.

"Observe and take notice, O Tegumai," said the Head Chief. "The Tribe of Tegumai have been fishing the Wagai river ever so long and ever so much too much. Consequence is, there's hardly any carp of any size left in it, and even the little carps are going away. What do you think of putting the big Tribal Tabu on it, so as to stop every one fishing there for six months?"

"That's a good plan, O Head Chief," said Tegumai. "But what will the consequence be if any of our people break tabu?"

"Consequence will be, O Tegumai," said the Head Chief, "that we will make them understand it with sticks and stinging-nettles and dobs of mud; and if that doesn't teach them, we'll draw fine, freehand Tribal patterns on their backs with the cutty edges of mussel-shells. Come along with me, O Tegumai, and we will proclaim the Tribal Tabu on the Wagai river."

Then they went up to the Head Chief's head house,

where all the Tribal Magic of Tegumai belonged; and they brought out the Big Tribal Tabu-pole, made of wood, with the image of the Tribal Beaver of Tegumai and the other animals carved on top, and all the Tribal Tabu-marks carved underneath.

Then they called up the Tribe of Tegumai with the Big Tribal Horn that roars and blores, and the Middle Tribal Conch that squeaks and squawks, and the Little Tribal Drum that taps and raps.

They made a lovely noise, and Taffy was allowed to beat the Little Tribal Drum, because she was rather friends with the Head Chief.

When all the Tribe had come together in front of the Head Chief's house, the Head Chief stood up and said and sang: "O Tribe of Tegumai! The Wagai river has been fished too much, and the carp-fish are getting frightened. Nobody must fish in the Wagai river for six months. It is tabu both sides and the middle; on all islands and mud-banks. It is tabu to bring a fishing-spear nearer than ten man-strides to the bank of the river. It is tabu, it is tabu, it is most 'specially tabu, O Tribe of Tegumai! It is tabu for this month and next month and next month and next month and next month and next month. Now go and put up the Tabu-pole by the river, and don't let anybody pretend that they haven't understood!"

Then the Tribe of Tegumai shouted, and put up the Tabu-pole by the banks of the Wagai river, and swiftly they ran down both banks (half the Tribe on one side and half on the other), and chased away all the small boys who hadn't attended the meeting because they were looking for crayfish in the river; and then they all praised the Head Chief and Tegumai Bopsulai.

Tegumai went home after this, but Taffy stayed with the Head Chief, because they were rather friends. She was very much surprised. She had never seen a tabu put on anything before, and she said to the Head Chief, "What does Tabu mean azactly?"

The Head Chief said, "Tabu doesn't mean anything till you break it, O Only Daughter of Tegumai; but when you break it, it means sticks and stinging-nettles and fine, freehand Tribal patterns drawn on your back with the cutty edges of mussel-shells."

Then Taffy said, 'Could I have a tabu of my own—a little small tabu to play with?'

Then the Head Chief said, "I'll give you a little tabu of your own, just because you made up that picture-writing, which will one day grow into the ABC." (You remember how Taffy and Tegumai made up the Alphabet? That was why she and the Head Chief were rather friends.)

He took off one of his magic necklaces—he had twenty-two of them—and it was made of bits of pink coral, and he said, "If you put this necklace on anything that belongs to you your own self, no one can touch that thing until you take the necklace off. It will only work inside your own Cave; and if you have left anything of yours lying about where you shouldn't, the tabu won't work till you have put that thing back in its proper place."

"Thank you very much indeed," said Taffy. "Now, what d'you truly s'pose it will do to my Daddy?"

"I'm not quite sure," said the Head Chief. "He may throw himself down on the floor and shout, or he may have cramps, or he may just flop, or he may take Three Sorrowful Steps and say sorrowful words, and then you can pull his hair three times if you like."

"And what will it do to my Mummy?" said Taffy.

"There aren't any tabus on people's Mummies," said the Head Chief.

"Why not?" said Taffy.

"Because if there were tabus on people's Mummies, people's Mummies could put tabus on breakfasts, and dinners, and teas, and that would be very bad for the Tribe. Long and long ago the Tribe decided not to have tabus on people's Mummies anywhere—for anything."

"Well," said Taffy, "do you know if my Daddy has any tabus of his own that will work on me— s'posin' I broke a tabu by accident?"

"You don't mean to say," said the Head Chief, "that your Daddy has never put any tabus on you yet?"

"No," said Taffy; "he only says 'Don't!' and gets angry."

"Ah! I suppose he thought you were a kiddy," said the Head Chief. "Now, if you show him that you've a real tabu of your own, I shouldn't be surprised if he put several real tabus on you."

"Thank you," said Taffy; "but I have a little garden of my own outside the Cave, and if you don't mind I should like you to make this tabu-necklace work so that if I hang it up on the wild roses in front of the garden, and people go inside, they won't be able to come out until they have said they are sorry."

"Oh, certainly, certainly," said the Head Chief. "Of course you can tabu your very own garden."

"Thank you," said Taffy; "and now I will go home and see if this tabu truly works."

When she got back to the Cave, it was nearly time for dinner; and when she came to the door, Teshumai Tewindrow, her dear Mummy, instead of saying, "Where have you been, Taffy?" said, "O Daughter of Tegumai, come in and eat," same as if she had been a grown-up person. That was because she saw a tabu-necklace on Taffy's neck.

Her Daddy was sitting in front of the fire waiting for dinner, and he said the very same thing, and Taffy felt most important.

She looked all round the Cave, to see that her own things (her private mendy-bag of otter-skin, with the shark's teeth and the bone needles and the deer-sinew thread; her mud-shoes of birch-bark; her spear and her throwing-stick and her lunch-basket) were all in their proper places, and then she slipped off her tabu-necklace quite quickly and hung it over the handle of the little wooden water-bucket that she used to draw water with.

Then her Mummy said to Tegumai, her Daddy, quite accidental, "O Tegumai! Won't you get us some fresh drinking-water for dinner?"

"Certainly," said Tegumai, and he jumped up and lifted Taffy's bucket with the tabu-necklace on it. Next minute he fell down flat on the floor and shouted; then he curled himself up and rolled round the cave; then he stood up and flopped several times.

"My dear," said Teshumai Tewindrow, "it looks to me as if you had rather broken somebody's tabu somehow. Does it hurt?"

"Horribly," said Tegumai. He took Three Sorrowful Steps and put his head on one side, and shouted, "I broke tabu! I broke tabu! I broke tabu!"

"Taffy, dear, that must be your tabu," said Teshumai Tewindrow. "You'd better pull his hair three times, or he will have to go on shouting till evening; and you know what Daddy is like when he once begins."

Tegumai stooped down, and Taffy pulled his hair three times; and he wiped his face, and said, "My Tribal Word! That's a dreadful strong tabu of yours, Taffy. Where did you get it from?"

"The Head Chief gave it me. He told me you'd have cramps and flops if you broke it," said Taffy.

"He was quite right. But he didn't tell you anything about Sign Tabus, did he?"

"No," said Taffy. "He said that if I showed you I had a real tabu of my own, you'd most likely put some real tabus on me."

"Quite right, my only daughter dear," said Tegumai. "I'll give you some tabus that will simply amaze you—Stinging-Nettle Tabus, Sign Tabus, Black and White Tabus—dozens of tabus. Now attend to me. Do you know what this means?"

Tegumai skiffled his forefinger in the air snakyfashion. "That's tabu on wriggling when you're eating your dinner. It is an important tabu, and if you break it, you'll have cramps—same as I did—or else I'll have to tattoo you all over."

Taffy sat quite still through dinner, and then Tegumai held up his right hand in front of him, the fingers close together. "That's the Still Tabu, Taffy. Whenever I do that, you must stop as you are, whatever you are doing. If you are sewing, you must stop with the needle halfway through the deer-skin. If you're walking, you stop on one foot. If you're climbing, you stop on one branch. You don't move until you see me go like this."

Tegumai put up his right hand, and waved it in front of his face two or three times. "That's the sign for Carry On. You can go on with whatever you are doing when you see me make that."

"Aren't there any necklaces for that tabu?" said Taffy.

"Yes. There is a red-and-black necklace, of course, but how can I come tramping through the fern to give you a Still Tabu necklace every time I see a deer or a rabbit, and want you to be quiet?" said Tegumai. "I thought you were a better hunter than that. Why, I might have to shoot an arrow over your head the minute after I had put Still Tabu on you."

"But how would I know what you were shooting at?" said Taffy.

"Watch my hand," said Tegumai. "You know the three little jumps a deer gives before he starts to run off—like this?" He looped his finger three times in the air, and Taffy nodded. "When you see me do that, you'll know we've found a deer. A little jiggle of the forefinger means a rabbit."

"Yes. Rabbits run like that," said Taffy, and jiggled her forefinger the same way.

"Squirrel's a long, climby-up twist in the air. Like this!"

"Same as squirrels kinking round trees. I see," said Taffy.

"Otter's a long, smooth, straight wave in the air—like this."

"Same as otters swimming in a pool. I see," said Taffy.

"And beaver's just as if I was smacking somebody with my open hand."

"Same as beavers' tails smacking on the water when they are frightened. I see."

"Those aren't tabus. Those are just signs to show you what I am hunting. The Still Tabu is the thing you must watch, because it's a big tabu."

"I can put the Still Tabu on, too," said Teshumai Tewindrow, who was sewing deer-skins together. "I can put it on you, Taffy, when you get too rowdy going to bed."

"What happens if I break it?" said Taffy. "You can't break a tabu except by accident." "But s'pose I did," said Taffy.

"You'd lose your own tabu-necklace. You'd have to take it back to the Head Chief, and you'd just be called Taffy again, not Daughter of Tegumai. Or perhaps we'd change your name to Tabumai Skellumzulai—the Bad Thing who can't keep a Tabu—and very likely you wouldn't be kissed for a day and a night."

"Umm!" said Taffy. "I don't think tabus are fun at all." "Well, take your tabu-necklace back to the Head Chief, and say you want to be a kiddy again, O Only Daughter of Tegumai!" said her Daddy. "No," said Taffy. "Tell me more about tabus. Can't I have some more of my very own—my very own—strong tabus that give people Tribal Fits?"

"No," said her Daddy. "You aren't old enough to be allowed to give people Tribal Fits. That pink necklace will do quite well for you."

"Then tell me more about tabus," said Taffy.

"But I am sleepy, daughter dear. I'll just put tabu on anyone talking to me till the sun gets behind that hill, and we'll go out in the evening and see if we can catch rabbits. Ask Mummy about the other tabus. It's a great comfort that you are a tabu-girl, because now I shan't have to tell you anything more than once."

Taffy talked quietly to her Mummy till the sun was in the right place. Then she waked Tegumai, and they both got their hunting things ready and went out into the woods. But just as she passed her little garden outside the Cave, Taffy took off her tabu-necklace and hung it on a rose-bush. Her garden-border was only marked with white stones, but she called the Rose the real gate into it, and all the Tribe knew it.

"Who do you s'pose you'll catch?" said Tegumai. "Wait and see till we come back," said Taffy. "The Head Chief said that anyone who breaks that tabu will have to stay in my garden till I let him out." They went along through the woods, and crossed the Wagai river on a fallen tree, and they climbed up to the top of a big bare hill where there were plenty of rabbits in the fern.

"Remember you're a tabu-girl now," said Tegumai, when Taffy began to skitter about and ask questions instead of hunting for rabbits; and he made the Still Tabu sign, and Taffy stopped as if she had been all turned into one solid stone. She was stooping to tie up a shoestring, and she stayed still with her hand on the string (We know that kind of tabu, don't we, Best Beloved?) only she looked hard at her Daddy, which you always must do when the Still Tabu is on. Presently, when he had walked a long way off, he turned round and made the Carry On sign. So she walked forward quietly through the bracken, always looking at her

Daddy, and a rabbit jumped up in front of her. She was just going to throw her stick, when she saw Tegumai make the Still Tabu sign, and she stopped with her mouth half open and her throwing-stick in her hand. The rabbit ran towards Tegumai, and Tegumai caught it. Then he came across the fern and kissed his daughter and said, "That is what I call a superior girldaughter. It's some pleasure to hunt with you now, Taffy."

A little while afterwards, a rabbit jumped up where Tegumai couldn't see it, but Taffy could, and she knew it was coming towards her if Tegumai did not frighten it; so she held up her hand, made the Rabbit Sign (so as he should know she wasn't in fun), and she put the Still Tabu on her own Daddy! She did—indeed she did, Best Beloved!

Tegumai stopped with one foot half lifted to climb over an old tree-trunk. The rabbit ran past Taffy, and Taffy killed it with her throwing-stick; but she was so excited that she forgot to take off the Still Tabu for quite two minutes, and all that time Tegumai stood on one leg, not daring to put his other foot down. Then he came and kissed her and threw her up in the air, and put her on his shoulder and danced and said, "My Tribal Word and Testimony! This is what I call having a daughter that is a daughter, O Only Daughter of Tegumai!" And Taffy was most tremenenssly and wonderhugely pleased.

It was almost dark when they went home. They

had five rabbits and two squirrels, as well as a water-rat. Taffy wanted the water-rat's skin for a purse. (People had to kill water-rats in those days because they couldn't buy purses, but we know that water-rats are just as much tabu, these particular days, for you and me as anything else that is alive.)

"I think I've kept you out a little too late," said Tegumai, when they were near home, "and Mummy won't be pleased with us. Run home, Taffy! You can see the Cave-fire from here."

Taffy ran along, and that very minute Tegumai heard something crackle in the bushes, and a big, lean, grey wolf jumped out and began to trot quietly after Taffy.

Now, all the Tegumai people hated wolves and killed them whenever they could, and Tegumai had never seen one so close to his Cave before.

He hurried after Taffy, but the wolf heard him, and jumped back into the bushes. Those wolves were afraid of grown-ups, but they used to try and catch the children of the Tribe. Taffy was swinging the water-rat and singing to herself—her Daddy had taken off all tabus—so she didn't notice anything.

There was a little meadow close to the Cave, and by the mouth of the Cave Taffy saw a tall man standing in her rose-garden, but it was too dark to make out properly.

"I do believe my tabu-necklace has truly caught somebody," she said, and she was just running up to look when she heard her Daddy say, "Still, Taffy! Still Tabu till I take it off!" She stopped where she was—the water-rat in one hand and the throwing-stick in the other—only turning her head towards her Daddy to be ready for the Carry On sign.

It was the longest Still Tabu she had had put upon her all that day. Tegumai had stepped back close to the wood and was holding his stone throwing-hatchet in one hand, and with the other he was making the Still Tabu sign.

Then she thought she saw something black creeping sideways at her across the grass. It came nearer and nearer, then it moved back a little and then it crawled closer.

Then she heard her Daddy's stone throwing-hatchet whirr past her shoulder just like a partridge, and at the same time another hatchet whirred out from her rose garden; and there was a howl, and a big grey wolf lay kicking on the grass, quite dead.

Then Tegumai picked her up and kissed her seven times and said, "My Tribal Word and Tegumai Testimony, Taffy, but you are a daughter to be proud of. Did you know what it was?"

"I'm not sure," said Taffy. "But I think I guessed it was a wolf. I knew you wouldn't let it hurt me."

"Good girl," said Tegumai, and he stooped over the wolf and picked up both hatchets. "Why, here's the Head Chief's hatchet!" he said, and he held up the Head Chief's magic throwing-hatchet, with the big greenstone head.

"Yes," said the Head Chief from inside Taffy's rosegarden, "and I'd be very much obliged if you would bring it back to me. I came to call on you this afternoon, and accidentally I stepped into Taffy's garden before I saw her tabu-necklace on the rose-tree. So, of course, I had to wait, till Taffy came back to let me out."

Then the Head Chief all in his feathers and shells took the Three Sorrowful Steps with his head on one side, and said, "I broke tabu! I broke tabu! I broke tabu!" and bowed solemnly and statelily before Taffy, till his tall eagle-feathers nearly touched the ground, and he said and he sang, "O Daughter of Tegumai, I saw everything that happened. You are a true tabu-girl. I am very pleased at you. At first I wasn't pleased, because I had to wait in your garden since six o'clock, and I know you only put tabu on your garden for fun."

"No, not fun," said Taffy. "I truly wanted to see if my tabu would catch anybody; but I didn't know that a little tabu like mine would work on a big Head Chief like you, O Head Chief."

"I told you it worked. I gave it to you myself," said the Head Chief. "Of course it would work. But I don't mind. I want to tell you, Taffy, my dear, that I wouldn't have minded staying in your garden from twelve o'clock instead of only six o'clock to see how beautifully you kept that last Still Tabu that your Daddy put on you. I give you my Chiefly Word, Taffy, that a great many men in the Tribe wouldn't have kept that tabu as you kept it, with that wolf crawling up to you across the grass."

"What are you going to do with the wolf-skin, O Head Chief?" said Tegumai, because any animal that the Head Chief threw his hatchet at belonged to the Head Chief by the Tribal Custom of Tegumai.

"I am going to give it to Taffy, of course, for a winter cloak, and I'll make her a magic necklace of her very own out of the teeth and claws," said the Head Chief; "and I am going to have the story of Taffy and the Still Tabu painted on wood on the Tribal Tabu-Count, so that all the girl-daughters of the Tribe can see and know and remember and understand."

Then they all three went into the Cave, and Teshumai Tewindrow gave them a most beautiful supper, and the Head Chief took off his eagle-feathers and all his necklaces; and when it was time for Taffy to go to bed in her own little cave, Tegumai and the Head Chief came in to say good-night, and they romped all round the cave, and dragged Taffy over the floor on a deer-skin (same as some people are dragged about on a hearth-rug), and they finished by throwing the otter-skin cushions about and knocking down a lot of old spears and fishing-rods that were hung on the walls. At last things grew so rowdy that Teshumai Tewindrow came in, and said, "Still! Still Tabu on every one of you! How do you ever expect that child to go to sleep?" And they said the really good-night, and Taffy went to sleep.

After that, what happened? Oh, Taffy learned all the tabus just like some people we know. She learned the White Shark Tabu, which made her eat up her dinner instead of playing with it (and that goes with a green-and-white necklace, you know); she learned the Grown-Up Tabu, which prevented her from talking when Neolithic ladies came to call (and, you know, a blue-and-white necklace goes with that); she learned the Owl Tabu, which prevented her staring at strangers (and a black-and-blue necklace goes with that); she learned the Open Hand Tabu (and we know a pure white necklace goes with that), which prevented her snapping and snarling when people borrowed things that belonged to her; and she learned five other tabus.

But the chief thing she learned, and the one that she never broke, not even by accident, was the Still Tabu.

That was why she was taken everywhere that her Daddy went.

# Preview
# The Dragon Lord's Secretary
# By Nicole Petit

*A special preview of Nicole Petit's debut novel,
The Dragon Lord's Secretary, available now
from 18thWall Productions*

*Dear Mr. Great and Glorious Dragon Lord,*
  *I am applying for a position you don't know that
you need filled, that of your secretary. Before you
reject this application, please consider the
following. Who organizes and polishes your
treasure hoard? Dragon claws are too large and
imprecise. You require an applicant with thumbs.
Who organizes your schedule? Dragons are too
self-interested for this work. You require an
applicant willing to write down your every meeting
and make sure each one fits neatly into your
calendar.*
  *I believe I am this applicant.*

*I come highly recommended, and I would gladly direct you to my previous employers. Unfortunately, most of them have died. Not through any misfortune or anything caused by me. They died of old age, as mortals tend to do. If you would like confirmation of my abilities, please contact Mr. Winston Churchill. He lives at 28 Hyde Park Gate, London, England, Mortal Realm.*

*I have enclosed my resume. It is very long. See the attached. (Inside the box. The huge box. You can't miss it.)*

*Sincerely,*
*Miss Scarlet Chase*

## Chapter 1

Deep in the land where magic hides, in the court of the Dragon Lord, a war as old as Camelot raged. Down past the caverns carved by dwarven hands, laced with streams of gold, fire blazed and armor clashed. Past the cavern halls smoke smudged the tableau. It seeped, black and riotous, from the mouths of slain guards. Roars shook the roots of the mountain.

In the throne room, a Knight brandished his shield against the mighty Dragon Lord.

Gales of wind from great black wings beat against the small body of the Knight. A wave of his hand and the mighty winds turned, slamming with greater force against the dragon's great head. The beast snarled, unveiling rows of sharp teeth.

"SUCH MAGIC DOES NOT IMPRESS ME, CHILD OF THE WIND."

Each rumbling word beat the Knight's armor; the force of sound slammed against his ribs.

"That was no magic, lizard. That was a warning. I've killed two of your kind today. Release your captive and you won't be the third."

The Dragon Lord circled the Knight.

"WARNINGS CARRY MORE WEIGHT WHEN YOU HOLD MORE THAN A SHIELD TO COWER BEHIND."

The golden blade attached to his whip-tail sliced through the shield and the power of its protective runes. The Knight howled, arm shattered by the force of the blow. The floor heaved beneath him as the dragon moved forward, each step causing tremors in the cave.

The jewel hung around the Dragon Lord's neck flared through the smoke. The massive gem was said to contain the flame of the very first dragon, a power more ancient than the entirety of the Knight's own race. The Dragon Lord towered over the fallen Knight, opening his jaws wide to call forth the ancient flame buried deep in his chest.

*CRACK!*

A whip made of the wind sliced through the roof of the Dragon Lord's mouth. Blood quenched the fire. The Dragon Lord reared back from his prey.

"Weight only burdens you, lead scales."

Blood continued to choke the Dragon Lord, but the fury boiling in his molten gold eyes said enough. Gold claws shot toward the Knight's chest. The Knight pulled back his whip and. . .

"I swear I leave the room for one hour and the whole place goes to pot."

From the secret tunnels behind the Dragon's Throne a young lady appeared. Curls of strawberry blonde hair escaped the tight bun and bounced across a pair of black rimmed glasses. Eyes the tangly green of spanish moss peered over the rims of her glasses. With a steady rhythm she tapped a pen against a notepad resting in one arm. The Dragon Lord stepped forward, his bloodied mouth hanging open. She gasped, resting the pen against her lips.

"Lord Almighty!"

The dragon smiled, his voice almost a purr. "Yes, Miss Chase?"

"Not *you*. The *merciful* one. Come down here, let me see." She crooked a finger. The dragon lowered his head, resting it against the floor. One slitted pupil kept a close watch on the Knight. The lady leaned in between his teeth, peering up at the wound. As she prodded experimentally with her pen the dragon writhed and snarled.

The Knight brandished his whip, "Step back, m'lady. I'll set you free from this beast."

Miss Chase pulled back, making notes on her notepad. "Beast is a horrible slur. It would be proper to call the Great and Glorious Dragon Lord Calix by his name, which just so happens to be the Great and Glorious Dragon Lord Calix. What, exactly, makes you think I need to be freed?"

The Knight stepped forward, laying a hand on her shoulder. His voice softened. "You're his slave."

She grimaced at the creases his armor made against her green blouse. With distaste she brushed off his heavy hand.

"Slave? Sir, I'm his secretary."

# Chapter 2

"And then you have a meeting with the Elder Wyrms For Wyvern Equality at three."

"LEVIATHAN BURN IT ALL! NOT THOSE WALKING CASES OF SCALE ROT."

Heaps of gold shuddered under the force of Calix's bellow. Priceless and highly breakable objects tumbled from their piles. The secretary sighed as she walked beside him, struggling to keep her hair in its bun as the wind whipped up by the Knight grew wilder and wilder.

"Would you mind taking this fight elsewhere? I *just* alphabetized the dwarven artifacts."

"PRIORITIES, MISS CHASE! MY KINGDOM IS IN PERIL!" A burst of flame scorched Calix's collection of Dragon-proof armor. He fled into the deeper reaches of the Dragon Lord's hoard. Calix chased after to be met with a crack of the whip against his muzzle. He roared, and a furious lash of his tail cast an entire pile of gold into the air. A flick of the secretary's wrist and the gold hung in the air.

Miss Chase arched a brow. "Peril? A single mage?"

"YES, PERIL! YOU LET ONE PEST IN AND AN INFESTATION IS SURE TO FOLLOW." He leaned down close and cleared his throat. "This would all be much easier if you would just let me eat him."

Miss Chase lowered her hand, the gold fell back into a neat pile. "Or, you know, I could just use my—"

"NO. I'M THE HOST, HE'S MY UNWANTED GUEST. I'LL DEAL WITH HIM, NOT YOU." With a lash of his wings the Dragon Lord slid off, scattering treasures as he went. Miss Chase sighed and made herself as comfortable as she could in a particularly rickety golden throne. The cavern shuddered. Gales of wind knocked over her carefully arranged vases, and plumes of fire displaced her organization. Dabbing the tip of her finger against her tongue she flipped through the pages on her notepad.

"Make it quick, my lord. You have a board meeting in an hour."

"BOARD MEETING? HELLHOUNDS TAKE YOU AND YOUR STRANGE PHRASEOLOGY, SECRETARY!"

A furious roar, a scattering of gold, and the Knight was launched high into the air by a swat from Calix's claws. His tail twitched merrily, molten gold eyes glittering at the sight. Instead of the clatter of armor against floor Calix expected, he was met with a furious blast of magic. Not the wind he had come to expect, but a more dazzling sort of shockwave that could only come from…

Miss Chase yelped and rushed through the thin paths, stopping at the section she reserved for cursed items. She came to a shield of some long forgotten race (knocked woefully out of place) and stopped. It was metallic with a milky white gloss, and shaped like a chrysalis' wing. Much too delicate for its purpose. Miss Chase stared at it, tracing the thin lines with her eyes. These lines pulsed with a silver light that she never recalled being there before. Confronted with a strange new glow in the cursed items section of Calix's hoard, she did what any self-respecting secretary would. She tapped on it with her pen.

The shield quivered, the lights pulsed bright. "IN THE NAME OF ALL THE OLD GODS OF ATLANTIS, WHERE AM I? WHAT HAVE YOU DONE TO ME, BEAST?"

Calix threw back his head and laughed, drowning out the Knight's cries. Miss Chase gave a resigned sigh, adding a note at the very bottom of her to-do list:

*Free Knight from cursed treasure.*

# Chapter 3

"Already here, my lord."

"Secretary, come at once!"

He rumbled, goblets and crowns tumbling off his sleek muzzle.

"The polite thing to do, mage, is to wait until after I call for you to answer."

A lopsided smile snuck across her lips. She tapped the tip of her pen against her temple. "You did call. It was just veeeeery slooooow getting from your head to your tongue. I was impatient."

A royal snort. "Do compose yourself."

She did. Calix sighed, a cloud of smoke puffed from his nostrils. It poured over the treasure, snaked toward Miss Chase and wrapped her in its heady cinnamon scent. He wormed deeper into the pile of gold and gems, stretching his long body. The enchanted shield that served as the Knight's prison bounced against his neck. The Knight had gone completely silent in the past few days, so naturally Calix decided he would make a good trophy necklace.

With a great sigh, he spoke. "Today I present

my glory to the grown hatchlings."

Miss Chase cocked her head, "Never heard you bemoan revealin' your glory before." She took a note on her notepad. Calix buried himself in his treasure, grumbling about "throwing gold before magi." A flick of her wrist and that gold tumbled off him, leaving his tender scales exposed to the elements. "Well, if it's such a trial, let's end your suffering swiftly."

Calix caught her up in his tail and set her between his wings. He set off with little ceremony. A cursory tip of the wings to his guards. He chuffed down the tunnels, where ancient dwarven runes were carved into the veins of glowing ore. He climbed up through crystal caverns shaped by countless scrapes of claws. Light shown at the end of the cavern, and he spread his wings. Out of his mountain home he soared, climbing high past the peak. A sharp turn had Miss Chase scrambling for a hold, as well as giving her a beautiful view of the kingdom below.

North, beyond the mountains crowned by Leviathan's Peak, stretched the Cracked Lands, a harsh desert from the days when an overeager sun scorched the new world, a home for exiles and wyverns only. To the south stretched the more temperate plains of Calix's domain, and newly founded mage-towns pushing against the dragons borders.

A quick twitch and Miss Chase was thrown from his back, plummeting to the ground far below. She yelped, mind sifting quickly through her options of spells. Wings pulled tight to his body, Calix dove steep. He laughed, twisting around her, carving tunnels into the sparse clouds. As the ground came up to meet them, his mighty wings flared and he settled on the edge of a cavern not far from his throne in Leviathan's Peak. He plucked his secretary out of the air with his tail and set her before him. She huffed, smoothed her blouse and skirt, and straightened her glasses. Catching her breath she stated, "Rather roundabout route, really."

Calix thrummed, head bobbing. "Need to stretch the wings now and then. Come, secretary, let me welcome you to our nests."

Close to the earth, the caverns went down, down, down. The tunnels were more humble, raked out by sharp claws, rubbed smooth by scales. Not a glint of gold or glow of crystal. The deeper they delved, the warmer it grew. A layer of dragon's smoke covered the ground; it issued from many dragons from what Miss Chase could tell by the mix of scents, each unique smoke belonging to an individual below. The heady scents began to overwhelm.

"Good Lord, it's like being in a candle store." She snapped her fingers and summoned a kerchief, tying it around her face.

Calix's scales bristled at the remark, "Enough of your strange words and insults, secretary. It's unwise to upset a nesting mother."

She cleared her throat, "Terr'bly sorry, sir. Your, er, incense is a bit too much for my shamefully inadequate schnoz."

Calix turned a golden eye on her. "You should come with a dictionary."

The tunnel gave way to hot springs, dragon's nests set as close to the warmth as manageable. The lanky lungs wrapped around their eggs, whiskers prickling and coils tightening as the secretary passed. They were larger and longer than Calix, and a mane of soft fur ran down their back. The lungs had no wings, but Miss Chase had come to recognize the tell-tale *swoosh* of one climbing through the sky like a snake through water.

Cohuatls perched on their high nests, eyeing the stranger. They were tubby winged snakes with stubby viper noses and spikey scales mixed with brilliant plumage. The cohuatls took a great deal of pride in the fact that they more closely resembled the mother of dragons, Aida the Rainbow Serpent, than the rest of their kind.

Calix and the rest of his kin were content to call themselves, simply, dragons. They came in a much wider variety of size and shape than the more pedigreed lungs and cohuatls. Some had great crests of horns, others delicate frills. There were thick builds and heavy plates of scales, and willowy sylphs who were nearly transparent.

Miss Chase sensed no hostility from the mothers, but there was no love lost here. She jotted down notes, unfazed. This was the typical reaction to her presence from any dragon who was not her boss. It was the hatchlings, too young to have left the nest, who bounded forward without a hint of reservation.

"Wow! A mage! Mother was right, Lord Calix does keep a pet."

Miss Chase crinkled her nose and peered over her glasses. "I'm no pet, I'm an employee."

The hatchlings blundered on. "Look at how it walks! Two legs!" cried a lung. She tried to copy the mage's walk, but tied herself in knots.

A cohuatl too young to fly slithered over, perching on her shoulders. "It's so small, I wonder how big they get!"

Another dragon tangled himself in her legs.

"I've heard they can spit water from their mouths!"

Miss Chase laughed. With more flourish than necessary she summoned an item none of the dragons had ever seen. Though the soft glint of bronze was enough to interest even the most cool eye. "Now y'all watch this, I'm a champion spitter. I'll land it right in that spittoon yonder." True to her word, the secretary shot an impressive spitball into the spittoon with a satisfying *ding!* The hatchlings crooned, staring up at her in awe. She stuck out her tongue for further inspection.

The cohuatl hatchling prodded experimentally with the tip of his tail then chirped. "Wet! Water! Oh no wonder the wyverns traded their fire—"

The adults hissed at the name of their sworn enemy, causing the hatchlings to cower. Before Miss Chase had time to intervene, the largest hot spring bubbled violently. From the depths burst a long neck and massive head, nearly three times the size of the Dragon Lord. Her smooth scales were dark as midnight, but with a rainbow sheen enhanced by the steam and water. She shared a crest of horns with the Dragon Lord, though hers were greater in number than the three on either side of Calix's head, as well as naturally dark without the ornaments of gold. Her eyes, though milky white, were sharp and searching. The nesting mothers all bowed low, murmuring respects to the "Great Wyrm."

"OH! MY DARLING SON HAS COME TO VISIT, HOW LOVELY! COME HERE, SWEET CHILD. LET ME SEE HOW MUCH YOU'VE GROWN. OH YOU ARE SUCH A HANDSOME YOUNG DRAKE." She crooned, her high voice booming.

The great Dragon Lord Calix shuffled his claws and burbled. Miss Chase rested her hands on her hips, "Now hold on, I've been with you for three years and never once have you brought me home to mother?"

The Great Wyrm bobbed her head, the dragon's version of a smile. "AND YOU MUST BE THE MAGE I HAVE HEARD SO MUCH OF, THE NEW PET OF CALIX. HOW DARLING! YOU EVEN GOT YOURSELF ONE OF THE SPECKLED ONES, CALIX. WHAT MAGIC DOES THIS ONE WIELD? THEY SAY SHE IS A SECRETARY. I HAVE NOT HEARD OF SUCH A SPECIALTY."

Attention turned off him, Calix regained his composure. He wound his neck around Miss Chase and looked her over. "Speckled? Hmmm. I thought they were blemishes." One of the hatchlings ventured near him and reached out to prod his tail. He grunted and swatted them away.

Miss Chase adjusted her glasses and assumed an

air of professionalism. "Ahem. They're freckles. Secretary, not pet, is my title. Empath is my specialty."

The Great Wyrm took this all in, head bobbing along. "OH HOW NICE. IT HAS BEEN HUNDREDS OF YEARS SINCE I'VE HAD THE PLEASURE OF A MAGE'S COMPANY, THOUSANDS SINCE ONE WAS AN EMPATH. SUCH A RARE TALENT FOR YOUR KIND. LAST ONE I KNEW GOT LOST IN A CAVE SOMEWHERE. I WONDER WHAT HAPPENED TO HIM. HMM, THIS WAR BETWEEN US DOES PUT A DAMPER ON RELATIONS, COLD AS IT MAY BE. TELL ME, DEAR, WHAT IS YOUR NAME?"

"Scarlet, Mrs.—er—Wyrm. Pleased to meetcha."

Calix thrummed at this. "Scarlet? I thought you were Miss Chase."

His secretary arched a brow. "Miss *Scarlet* Chase, to be exact."

Calix growled. "You never told me your name was Scarlet."

"Three years and you never bothered to ask. Or read my resume."

Two hatchlings gathered the courage to approach the Dragon Lord, distracting him from the conversation. A warning growl sent them scurrying away.

The Wyrm thrummed. "I DON'T BLAME YOU, DEAR, FOR MISSING THE ELDER WYRMS FOR WYVERN EQUALITY MEETING WITH SUCH A LOVELY LITTLE COMPANION."

Scarlet's eyes widened. "Waitwaitwait. You're one of the 'walking cases of scale rot'?"

"OH IS THAT WHAT WE'RE CALLED THESE DAYS?" She thrummed, almost a chuckle. "YES, LITLE ONE, I'M THE HEAD OF IT!"

Scarlet threw back her head and laughed. She smacked Calix's snout. "You never told me your *mom* was a part of this."

A crowd of the hatchlings wound their way between Calix's legs. His fangs came down like guillotines, and his tail lashed. He whirled around, wreathing himself in smoke and flame. He reared up, wings flared wide, and the first embers of dragonfire kindled. The hatchlings froze, curling tails tight around themselves. He roared, and what followed shook the mountain's roots.

"YOU THINK YOU ARE TO BE CONGRATULATED? YOU THINK YOU ARE DRAGONS?" He curled his claws into the rock and it came up as dust. "YOU ARE MERE LIZARDS. NO FLIGHT, NO FIRE, UNWORTHY OF MY NOTICE."

Scarlet recoiled, clutching at her head.

The Great Wyrm chuffed. "NOW THAT'S NOT

VERY KIND OF YOU, CALIX. SCARING THE HATCHLINGS, GIVING YOUR EMPATH A HEADACHE. THEY'RE ALL VERY SENSITIVE, YOU KNOW."

The rest of the squabble was lost on Scarlet, her mind seared by the Dragon Lord's sudden rage. She stumbled back, dazed, tripped on a dragon's claw and fell down onto its foot. The nesting mother lashed her tail and batted Scarlet away. Scarlet's glasses fell, a lense popped out and cracked. The dragons not involved with Calix's display turned to watch. Scarlet brushed herself off and held up her hands.

"It's okay, I don't need 'em anyway. I just use those to look smart."

"Your kind is the reason mine are so small in number. Your kind pushes against our borders. We are at war with you. Why our lord keeps you here I do not know—"

"To be fair, it's a cold war. You stopped burning towns and they stopped building more. You stopped kidnapping nobles and Knights stopped coming to take 'em back. Y'all just kinda glare at eachother from a distance, and sometimes you eat their sheep. And me, well, the big fella keeps me because I can type a solid eighty-five words per minute, no mistakes. I'm not even slowed by the typewriter's carriage bar because magic—"

"Go back to your towns and burn." Flames licked the edges of her fangs, neck arched back in preparation to strike.

Scarlet arched a brow. "Now, that's just rude."

A flash of midnight scales wrapped in bronze. Aurum had come. Radiant Raider of the Cracked Lands, Herald of the Dragon Lord. She pounced on the nesting mother, wrapping her lithe body around the larger dragon. The nesting mother bellowed as Aurum's needle claws dug into the spots where scales did not protect. She didn't roar, she hissed through a snarl. "You dare slight the great Lord of Dragons in his very presence? I should kill you now."

Calix grew quiet and turned toward his Herald. Aurum's words caused the other dragons to shudder.

The Great Wyrm chuffed. "DEATH IS A HEFTY PRICE, AURUM, FOR HER AND US. WE ARE SO FEW IN NUMBER NOW, AND OUR CLUTCHES SMALL. I TAUGHT YOU AND ALL HERE NOT TO KILL YOUR OWN KIND."

Aurum tightened her coils. "You taught me our laws. You know that such a slight against the reigning lord is a killing offense."

Scarlet dashed forward. "Woah, woah, hold on.

She didn't insult him, it was me she was after. No need to throw the death penalty around now."

Aurum snorted. "You belong to the Dragon Lord. To slight you is to affront him. But you're right, you mean little in the great scheme of things. I shall show mercy and rip her wings off instead."

The mother writhed. "No, please! Don't bring such shame on my house. I would rather you kill me swiftly."

A shudder passed through the stumps where Aurum's wings should have been. Her eyes narrowed. "I bear the shame just fine, wretch. And so will you." She opened her jaws wide, arched her neck high, and...

Twitched.

Her bronze eyes turned toward Scarlet. "I feel you in my mind, mage," she spat. "Release your hold on me now. Let me do my job."

The secretary's face had hardened, nearly a match for the Radiant Raider. "No. I can't let you do that. It's not right."

Aurum hissed. "Calix, you let this mage speak too freely. Shut her mouth."

Calix kept silent and still, eyes half lidded, face inscrutable.

It was the Great Wyrm who intervened. "AURUM, MY CHILD, PLEASE. STEP DOWN."

Scarlet released her hold on Aurum's mind. The raider loosed her coils and slithered toward Calix's side. She looked him over and chuffed. "It's not wise, Lord, to let a mage speak for you. It casts a bad image to your subjects. Some might think you grow too attached to her."

Calix didn't bother to glance her way. "She does not speak for me, Raider. Neither do you."

Aurum's crest of spines bristled, she snapped her fangs but held her tongue.

Calix turned to his secretary. "Aurum, my right wing, my sister, has a right to dispense justice in my name. You dared to stand in her way because you claim this isn't right. Well then, mage, since you certainly know best—" he chuffed "—what do you propose we do?"

Scarlet swallowed. All eyes were on her now. The nesting mother towered over her small form, waiting. Scarlet sighed. "Well, I guess we can't just let bygones be bygones." A negative rumble from the crowd confirmed that. "Alright then, uh, I heard about a time when the clever Aida punished a boastful Leviathan by binding his mouth."

Scarlet made a gesture much like tying a knot. The nesting mother jerked back and flared her wings, but her jaw stayed shut. Scarlet turned toward Calix, bowing. "Erm, if that's all pleasing to you, my lord."

Calix thrummed. "It would be unwise to refuse the wisdom of the first dragons, Miss...Scarlet." He rose, flaring his wings and arching his neck. "My secretary will free you in a week's time, by then I'll hope you'll have learned the benefits of a closed mouth." He snapped his jaws, a burst of flame licking his fangs.

He turned and headed toward the exit. "Come, secretary, I've spent enough time here as it is."

As Scarlet hurried to keep up with him, she heard the Great Wyrm call, "WHEN YOU RETURN, CALIX, I'LL HAVE SOME WORDS WITH YOU ABOUT THE PROPER SPEECH TO GIVE A HATCHLING."

Calix growled and lashed his tail, ducking into the caverns. When they were safely out of range, he slowed and allowed his secretary to take her place at his side. He lowered his head to her level as he wormed along, studying her with one golden eye. "I was mistaken to think three years was enough to uncover all the secrets of a mage, Miss Scarlet."

Her lips twitched. "A first name and fake glasses, I'm just full of surprises."

Calix might have retorted if the shield around his neck hadn't interrupted. It rattled, the silver light pulsed. From within, the Knight spoke.

"It won't be our towns burning when the Firetail comes."

Calix chuffed and swatted at the shield. "Rather delayed comeback, Child of Wind." He looked back up to find Scarlet frozen, eyes wide and face pale.

# Preview
# The Curious Case of the Clockwork Doll
# By Heidi J. Hewett

*The thrilling January release in 18thWall
Productions' The Science of Deduction*

*221b Baker Street has never lacked for visitors.
Princes and kings, washerwomen and
governesses, the lost and the liars. But never one
such as this.*

*But in the final days of the Boer War, Sherlock
Holmes receives a most unexpected guest. A
serving girl, whose clothes are ten years out of
date and speaks in repeated phrases. She answers
any question put to her with mathematical
exactitude. More shocking is the secret hidden
under her bonnet...*

*As Sherlock Holmes contends with this case, he
must confront a master thief, a supposed ghost,
uncommon butlers, miraculous engines Charles
Babbage never dreamed of, and the impact of a
war on the far side of the globe.*

## Chapter One

Among the many startling successes of Mr. Sherlock Holmes' career are a few unavoidable failures—not all of the cases presented to Holmes have resulted in a happy conclusion, as I observed in my account of *The Adventure of the Solitary Cyclist*. There have been occasions on which my friend exerted his great deductive powers of reasoning to unravel a mystery, and yet we arrived too late to prevent a tragedy.

I have noted that the period between 1894 and 1901 was one of the busiest for my friend, for he consulted in many public cases and hundreds of private cases of the most intricate and extraordinary character. Records of these cases, illustrating the curious problems presented to Mr. Holmes, are kept in the vaults of the bank of Cox and Co., but most have never been made known to the public.

One in particular concerned services to the crown which I was at the time unable to describe, being obliged as a partner and confidant to avoid any indiscretion. The whole affair was so carefully hushed up in the interests of national security that few, if any, know the events I am about to relate. But seeing that the South African war is long over, and it has been years since the Haviland name has been heard in England, it is perhaps as well that the true details of this inconceivable affair should now come to light.

The year was 1900. Holmes was, at the time, involved in the investigation of the theft of a rare and valuable artwork, a blackmail case, and the search for a washer-woman's lost brother, which, he said, was likely to prove the most interesting of the three. We were, however, only moderately engaged that particular morning, and Holmes, as usual, was dividing his time between his endless scrap-booking and the chemical experiments in which he took pleasure, while I reclined with my pipe in the old cane-backed chair in our little flat. The *Daily Telegraph* had slipped from my hands, and I was sitting, smoking meditatively, when my companion's voice interrupted the reverie into which I had fallen.

"Indeed, Watson," said he, still looking through the eyepiece of the microscope on the acid-stained, deal-topped table. "Of all of man's inventions, war is the most terrible. Pindar was right: there is a great difference between the idea and the fact."

I bolted upright in my chair in surprise. "But this is marvelous, Holmes! How could you have known what was in my thoughts just now?"

Holmes straightened and spun around on his

stool. There was a mischievous twinkle in his eye. "I have demonstrated to you before that it is possible to read another's mind, if one has sufficient skill in observation."

"But how could you know I was thinking of that particular quote from Pindar?" I protested. "You have had your back turned to me, and I have been sitting here this entire time, with only my newspaper."

Holmes waved aside my objection. He crossed the room to the fireplace, and selecting a favorite long-stemmed pipe from the coal-scuttle, he began:

"The newspapers have been full of reports of the surrender of Pretoria in the Transvaal, and the expectation is that now that the capital has fallen, the war will soon be over—have you the tobacco-slipper? Ah! I see it next to you. If you would be so kind as to toss it to me. Thank you!—Yet earlier this morning you were telling me the Boers have taken up a defensive position in the hills. You speculated that our side could not afford to ignore the threat to rearward communications, and further action would be necessary."

Using the fire-tongs, he lit his pipe from a coal in the grate and resumed:

"Just now, your old wound caused you

momentary discomfort, and you thought back to the hardships which soldiers must endure: extremes of temperature, scarcity of food and supplies, fever, dysentery. In the reflection of the tea-pot, I observed you adjust your collar as if you felt warm and guessed that you were remembering your experiences among the Afghans.

"The futility of it—so many men sick and dying—struck you as you considered that Britain's interest in the region stems from an insatiable desire for diamonds and gold, which are plentiful in those parts, and your expression changed into one of disgust. It so happened then that a man passing in the street below chanced to whistle a phrase from the old war song, 'By Jingo,' and again you felt a patriotic stirring."

"I didn't even hear the man whistling!"

"Nevertheless, your mind took in the sensation. You sat up straighter in your chair. You remembered that Britain has an obligation to protect its colonists; that we have a moral duty to intervene on behalf of the black Africans whom the Boers enslave.

"Your eye chancing to fall upon an open book of Horace, you recalled his famous exhortation— for the undirected mind runs down habitual paths—that it is sweet and glorious to die for one's country. This quotation immediately put you in mind of another by Pindar: 'War is sweet to those who have never experienced it.' I then remarked that I heartily agreed with you and you were amazed." He blew out a cloud of smoke.

"So that was all there was to it!" I said, slapping my thigh and laughing heartily. "Astonishing, Holmes! Why, you have laid the whole mystery bare, like the tumbler mechanism of a lock or the inner working of my pocket-watch! I thought at first there was something to it, but a child could see it now."

"Yes," said my friend with a note of bitterness, turning away. "The spectator is overcome with amazement when the magician pulls away the curtain to reveal the final result, but let him draw aside that curtain and show the steps by which that result is accomplished, and the spectator dismisses the achievement as nothing more than a cheap trick. So the chain of deductive reasoning laid out seems, retrospectively, a simple feat."

As my friend was speaking, I had shifted my position to the window-seat of our little flat, and happening to glance down into the street, I observed a lady heavily-veiled and dressed in black stepping out of a hansom cab.

Holmes joined me at the window. "It appears we

have a client," he remarked, studying her through a parting in the curtain. "You see, she does not hesitate."

I saw her give the driver eight and sixpence without a word, and the hansom clattered away as she turned back to our door.

"The second half of a first class return ticket," Holmes said, snapping his magnifying lens shut and replacing it in his breast pocket. "The lady's clothes and carriage bespeak elegance, but her shoes are wrong. Someone who has been fairly well-to-do previously, but now lives within reduced circumstances. That bonnet, like an upside-down flower-pot, trimmed with a hideous assortment of feathers, hasn't been seen for ten years in London."

Just then, the lady in the street below glanced upward. Her eyes were hidden behind the veil, but she gazed so fixedly at the very spot where we stood that I was possessed by the uncomfortable sensation she had overheard our conversation.

I retreated from the window to stand behind the armchair.

"Now, Holmes, how could you possibly know about the fashion of ladies hats?"

Holmes let the curtain slip from his fingers. "It is my business to observe such small details. You remember the Abernetty case; everything of importance hinged on the parsley in the butter dish."

"She is clearly a woman of good character and birth," I said, recalling the graceful turn of the ankle as she stepped down from the hansom.

"I draw only such deductions as can be made from the evidence before me. She may be an axe murderer who has drowned babies and strangled cats."

"Holmes, you are a machine, an absolute machine! Have you no feeling at all?"

"It is a maxim of mine that women are never to be entirely trusted. The most winning woman of my acquaintance murdered three innocent children for their insurance-money. It is best not to let one's tender emotions cloud the superior function of the Intellect."

We heard the sharp clang of the bell, and a moment later our long-suffering housekeeper and landlady, Mrs. Hudson, gently rapped upon the door and announced, "There is a woman down below to see you, sir."

"A woman, and not a lady? Well, well! Ask her to step up." Turning to me, Holmes continued, chuckling, "We shall see if we can detect what the excellent Mrs. Hudson has observed about our visitor."

There was a bustle outside on the landing, and Mrs. Hudson opened the door to usher in our guest.

She was, as I have mentioned, dressed in black silk under a traveling cloak, with an outmoded and unattractive hat. She wore black leather gloves, and her face was completely covered by a thick lace veil, so that it was difficult at first sight to say more than that she carried herself with dignity, and her voice, when she spoke, was exceedingly gentle and pleasant.

"Have I the honor of addressing, Mr. Sherlock Holmes?"

"And my associate, Doctor Watson," he said, waving in my direction and gesturing for her to take a seat. "There is nothing that can be said to me which cannot be said before him."

She turned toward me and inclined her head.

"And what brings you to London, Miss—?" my friend began, as I discreetly slipped out my pocket note-book.

"Haviland," said she. "My name is Martha Haviland."

"And you have a matter, Miss Haviland, on which you desire to consult me?"

"I have come on behalf of Miss Judith

Haviland," she said. "She is the mistress of the Haviland estate. She would much value your advice regarding a succession of strange incidents that have occurred in connection with the house."

"I am all attention," said Holmes, casting himself into a chair and closing his eyes. "Pray give us the essential facts, and afterward I can question you as to any relevant details you may have missed."

"I will tell you what Miss Haviland wished me to tell you, that lately the family has been subject to the whims of an unseen force: capricious, sometimes malevolent. Small articles disappear or are discovered to have been moved. Drawers are opened. Some in the household report hearing noises in the passageways. Even at times, a cold touch has been felt." The veiled woman seated on the sofa fell silent, and I wondered who she was that she referred to Miss Haviland in this oblique way. Surely, I thought to myself, Mrs. Hudson must be mistaken. A poor relation of the Havilands, perhaps, but her speech and bearing suggested refinement of character and breeding.

"The family—" Holmes prompted. "Who lives in the house?"

"There is Miss Judith Haviland, Mr. Lionel Haviland, her brother, a nursery governess named

Miss Berends, and her charge, Mary Haviland."

"And it is *Miss* Haviland to whom the property belongs?" I ventured. "That certainly is unusual."

The veiled woman made a curious yet graceful gesture, a half-circle of the wrist as if to say, *I cannot tell.*

"And the house?" Holmes questioned her. "Who else has access to the house? How is it situated?"

"We live a private, retired life," the woman said in her clear, measured voice. "The house in Sussex is remotely placed. We never see anyone except the occasional tradesman from the village."

"Then it is one of the servants," Holmes said, sitting up and opening his eyes without interest. "I suggest you recommend to Miss Haviland that she make a thorough inspection and give notice to the offender at once."

"One moment," I interjected, and the woman turned her head toward me. "You said, 'sometimes malevolent.'"

My friend had wandered to the mantelpiece and pulled down one of his reference books. "Haviland the inventor?" he asked over his shoulder.

The woman inclined her head.

"Has the ghost an identity?" I asked.

Again, the curious gesture of the wrist. "I do not know. Can you say more?"

"I have heard," I began cautiously, "that a ghostly visitation may betoken some unfinished business, even a cry for help."

"I am not aware. Can you say more?" she asked sweetly.

"Well," said I, becoming confused, "I mean to ask, does it have a name, this ghost? Is there any indication of its motive, why it is haunting this particular family or house?"

"I do not know. Can you say more?"

My friend interrupted in that brusque manner he sometimes chooses to adopt: "Good day, Miss Martha. Mrs. Hudson will see you out. You have had a long journey to London to no avail. I regret the trouble you have taken to see me," said he, turning his back and snapping the book shut.

The woman rose without a word and started toward the door, when, in one of those mercurial shifts of temper that characterized my friend, Holmes pivoted and called after her: "Do not go yet, Miss Martha. Please," he held out his hand, indicating her former seat. "There are one or two points in connection with your case not entirely devoid of interest. I beg you will continue."

"I have reported everything as Miss Haviland directed."

"Tell me, Miss Martha, how many miles is it

from Eastbourne to London?" Holmes asked.

"73.2," was the prompt reply.

"And how many stops between Eastbourne and Victoria Station?"

"19."

"How much is 37,250 times 987?" A wild light was shining in Holmes' eyes and his tone had taken on a sportive, almost malicious quality.

She seemed about to speak, but stopped short, sensing a trap.

*"As I was going to St. Ives, I met a man with seven wives,"* Holmes began to ramble to my astonishment:

*"Each wife had seven sacks,*
*Each sack had seven cats,*
*Each cat had seven kits:*
*Kits, cats, sacks, and wives,*
*How many were there going to St. Ives?*

"Oh, glorious! Glorious!" he concluded, crowing with sudden laughter. "No! Pray, don't go, Miss Martha. You are among friends!" He flapped his hands toward her in his excitement, urging her to make haste. "Pray, be uncovered! Pray, remove your veil."

# Chapter Two

It was a face to rival the beauties of the day, with delicately formed lips, a small chin, high cheekbones, shapely brows, and large dark eyes hidden modestly behind lashes. Her countenance was at once child-like and womanly, of equal parts innocence and grace.

The skin was not like true skin, for Art cannot so perfectly replicate Nature, and I now understood why she wore gloves, else her hands should have given her away at once. The skin was without blemish, of a pale and rosy hue, and yet, I say, it filled me with revulsion and horror. She saw my look and paused in pinning up her veil. She turned her eyes full upon me then, and I saw that the aqueous orbs had the curiously flat quality of a being that possesses life, but no soul.

Holmes had crossed the room in a few quick steps and stood, hovering with barely contained excitement over the couch.

"You will permit…I am a student of Phrenology." Holmes carefully lifted the hat and set it aside. "The catch? Ah!" He exclaimed with a cry of satisfaction as it gave way.

Through a small square aperture we gazed down

into Martha's brain. The horror of my previous impression was surpassed only by my wonder at what I beheld: a gelatinous blue sea encased in a bubble of glass finer and more fragile in appearance than that of an electrical bulb, in which floated a thousand sparks of light, rather say a thousand thousands, or more, for they were beyond numbering, like tiny signal ships winking to one another. Or perhaps it would be better to compare them to those strange, luminescent fish rumoured to live in the deepest part of the ocean, for the flashes did not merely float on the surface but appeared embedded in the blue jelly. Underneath, the dim outline of a small rectangular plate could be seen, from which a tangle of filaments descended, not unlike the nerves of a body. Some of the nerve filaments snaked away to microscopic metal discs embedded upon the inner surface of the outer visage, which was supported by a contoured scaffolding of tiny metal struts. Thicker cords of wires, twisted together like fibers of rope, fed into the brain from the eye and ear sockets.

"An automaton!" I exclaimed in breathless admiration.

"Most remarkable," Holmes murmured.

"I have never seen anything like it," I said. We both spoke in whispers. At each sound we uttered, flashes darted through the jelly, almost too quick for the human eye, momentarily lighting up a fantastical forest of miniature trees with a million forked branches and fading out of sight.

"But how did you know?" I asked.

"Descartes noted that by their nature, automata may appear to respond to stimuli, but are unable to produce variety of linguistic response, which simple questioning quickly reveals. You observed, no doubt, the repeated gestures and turns of phrase. I recognized the Haviland family name, which first set my thinking along these lines."

"Are you in any discomfort, Miss Martha?" I inquired.

"None," she replied, "I must return home before my electrical reserves are depleted."

I had heard of German and French experiments with batteries made of zinc and carbon, but this must have been something superior in sophistication. I glanced at the seated form, in so many respects identical to the genuine article, and wondered where her supply of power was housed. Did it replace the heart? One of the organs of digestion?

Holmes replaced the covering with a small sigh of regret. I think he would have liked to dissect her then and there if he had known where to start, but she was a creature far beyond either of our capabilities or experience.

"You may tell Miss Haviland," he said, addressing the automaton, "that we will take her case. I have one or two other cases at hand of some importance which require my presence in London, but she may expect us Wednesday next. A day in the country will do me no harm. Watson, I should be glad of your company, if you can spare the time."

I held the door open for her, and Miss Martha, for so I persisted in thinking of her, passed through, giving me a small, courteous nod, for all the world like a real woman of flesh and blood. It was so completely natural that I unthinkingly wished her good day. Closing the door, I turned and saw Holmes' smile.

"I dare say you thought I acted rather badly to Miss Martha just now?"

"I have learned to trust your judgment."

"Very sensible, Watson. And now as there is nothing more to be done, I shall devote myself to Hoffmann. If you would be so good as to consult Bradshaw near your elbow—I believe there is a train from Victoria at two o'clock—and ask Mrs. Hudson to send up dinner."

Holmes took up the violin from its case in the

corner, and a few moments later the haunting notes of the barcarole could be heard throughout our apartment.

Holmes sat opposite me, for we had the first-class carriage to ourselves, and busied himself with *Le Figaro* as the train steamed southward. We had hardly passed Keymer Junction, however, before he cast it aside and sat drumming his fingers.

I looked up from the *Chronicle*. "Well, victory for our boys at Diamond Hill. The Boers will have no choice but to surrender to Roberts now, I think."

"Who?"

"Surely you are joking!" I exclaimed. "Field Marshal Frederick Roberts? Commander-in-Chief of the Forces? Why just the other day I was telling you about his capture of Pretoria. Those brave fellows are fighting for Britain out there. You might try to care."

"Crime is my business," my friend replied in his curt manner. "I am a brain, to which the rest of this," he gestured carelessly, "body, is mere appendage. The detection and unraveling of crime is my great purpose, toward which all my mental energies are devoted. I cannot afford to stuff my head with useless facts in the haphazard way you do, Watson."

I raised one eyebrow and retreated behind my newspaper.

Holmes continued to stare out the window over the landscape. We were still too far north on the line to see the Downs or the chalky cliffs of the coast, but the countryside was pleasant and dotted with small farms.

"Quite a change from the gloom of London, is it not, Watson?" Holmes mused gloomily. "Perhaps I shall one day withdraw into retirement. I will settle myself in some secluded spot like this and devote myself to the study of bees. Don't you miss it already? London? The great metropolis, riddled with factories and workshops. The docks swarming with trade from the far reaches of the Empire. Six million souls seething with activity as their individual ends direct them, fueling conflict and crime. There is food for the mind, exercise for one's talent!

"Well, well," he concluded sourly. "I shall investigate this paltry 'ghost' of the Havilands. There is quite enough ordinary evil to go around without invoking supernatural interference. But Martha," Holmes stopped and chuckled quietly to himself. "Martha interests me very much."

"It still fills me with wonder that such a thing is

possible," I said. "How on earth did you work it out?"

"I recognized Haviland's name from my scrapbook in connection with a case I worked in '78—before your time, old fellow—for the French modeller, Tavernier. Haviland used to manufacture clockwork apparatus for him when his work called for it. I saw some of his early inventions, but nothing, nothing like this. I believe he has been dead now some five years.

"The estate belonged at one time to one of the wealthiest families in England, but mismanagement and neglect through successive generations reduced it to a shadow of its former self. In 1885 Haviland announced he was retiring from public life and retreated into this venerable wreckage of aristocratic poverty. The years passed. The great inventor produced nothing, and saw no one. His reputation crumbled, and it was whispered about that he had inherited the strain of insanity which runs in his family.

"I now believe that Arthur Haviland was, in fact, at work on his greatest invention of all—an invention so astounding it defies belief—and that his mania for secrecy prevented him from making it known. The Havilands are indeed a very private family, but I recall hearing that the son, Lionel, has, at a young age, learned to play heavily at cards and squander money on the turf."

While he was speaking, Holmes had taken out his pipe, which he laid across his knees, and he felt in his breast-pocket. "Perhaps that is the reason he has been disinherited in favor of the sister. Have you a match?"

I had not. "I'll go in search of the porter," said I and stepped out into the corridor. Before I had taken two strides, the connecting door at the far end of the carriage was flung open with great force, and a barrel-chested man with a cap pulled low over his eyes burst through, clutching a small case.

I stood my ground, prepared to block his progress, but he pulled down the window of the rushing train as it neared a bend in the track and flung the case down the embankment.

"Stop there!" I cried, and the man looked up at me. Just then, the conductor came through, shouting, "Thief!"

I heard the sharp, shrill sound of the brakes, and the train lurched to a stop.

# Chapter Three

With a snarl the man pushed violently past me and disappeared through the connecting door behind me into the next car. I staggered to my feet as the conductor ran up.

"Are you all right, sir?"

"Fine, fine." I waved him on. "He threw a small case out that window."

The conductor stuck his head out of the window and looked back. The train had now come to a stop, just short of the Lewes Station. "I see it, sir." He took out his whistle and signaled to one of his fellows.

I returned to our compartment.

"There has been some excitement," I said. "Someone on this train appears to have been robbed. The thief must have panicked when the alarm was given and tossed the goods. I did my best to stop him, but the ruffian was too strong for me."

"You are unhurt?"

"Only my pride was injured," I explained ruefully.

"Well, well," Holmes said. "Hello! Here is a familiar face." ✦

A moment later, the door to our compartment slid open, and Inspector Lestrade thrust his head inside.

"Ah, Mr. Holmes! I might have guessed you'd be mixed up in this business."

Holmes had sunk back against the cushions, and he surveyed the Scotland Yard detective with a languid, half-smile. "I assure you I am perfectly innocent of any involvement. Pray, enlighten me."

Lestrade's ferret-like eyes narrowed. "You mean you're not here on the trail of Jack of Diamonds?"

"Certainly not. I have been engaged by a client in the vicinity of Fulworth on an entirely separate matter. What is this Jack of Diamonds supposed to have done?"

Lestrade's manner changed entirely. "Well, then, Mr. Holmes. Seeing as you're here, and that you have been of assistance to us on the Force once or twice before...."

I coughed.

Holmes modestly waved Lestrade's understatement aside and indicated that the inspector should be seated.

Lestrade took off his hat and sat down. "We had an anonymous tip there might be a robbery on this line."

"Watson here saw the thief," Holmes said.

Lestrade turned to me with interest. "Did you now? And do you think you could describe him?"

"Well," I said hesitantly as Lestrade pulled out his note-book. "It was only a brief moment, but I should say he was middle-size, a strongly built man. Rather a thick neck, square jaw, moustache."

"Square jaw, moustache. Right." Lestrade tapped his pencil against the page.

Holmes chuckled. "Why, my dear Watson, you have just described half the men in England. Middle-size? A moustache?"

"A disguise?"

"Undoubtedly."

"Disguise or no disguise, we'll catch him. We have him dead to rights this time," Lestrade said with grim triumph. "The lady's maid raised the alarm as soon as she saw the jewel case was missing. The conductor says he happened to notice a furtive-looking man and followed him. When he called out to him to stop, the thief broke into a run, but the conductor says, except when his view was blocked between the carriages, he had him in sight. My men are going through the train now. It's a matter of time before we identify him."

"I should advise then that you look for a man without a moustache," Holmes said.

"He can't hide forever," Lestrade said. "He's on this train. We've got him and the jewels this time."

"Excuse me, sir." A plainclothes detective, sweating profusely, tapped on the glass and entered our compartment, bearing a small, black case.

"That's the one," I said, pointing to it.

Holmes suppressed a smile. "Your ability to identify a carrying case is somewhat better than your ability to identify the man who took it."

"We've searched the train," the plainclothes man said. "We found this down the embankment."

Lestrade was wrestling with the case. "It's locked."

"Here, sir. Lady Kildaire gave me the key."

Lestrade inserted the key and turned it in the lock. The case opened with a snap.

"He's done it again," Lestrade growled, tossing the jewel case onto the seat beside him.

I looked into the velvet folds of the interior. The case was empty.

Holmes bent forward to pick up the red and white playing card that had drifted to the floor and turned it over in his hands. "The Jack of Diamonds. Our mysterious friend has also been busy on the Continent," Holmes remarked. "Vienna last month. Paris before that. Prague two weeks ago. I recognized the *modus operandi* at once."

"You've been following this case?" I asked.

"Only incidentally. I read the papers, my dear Watson, just as you do, but to greater purpose."

"I'm surprised you haven't taken more of an interest in this business," said Lestrade.

Holmes shrugged. "As the poet says, *'Who steals my purse steals trash; 'tis something, nothing; 'Twas mine, 'tis his…'* Every jewel of real value has a long and bloody history. And Lady Kildaire is not my client. Still, the solution is obvious, is it not?"

"Oh, so you've solved the case already, have you?" Lestrade said bitterly.

"I have told you it is not my affair."

"Wait," I interjected. "I think I have it. What if there were two cases.… This Jack fellow steals one and passes it to his accomplice on the train, who substitutes a second, empty case, which Jack then tosses out the window?"

"No, no," Lestrade interrupted. "Say Jack grabs the goods, tosses them out the window. Then his accomplice nabs the real jewel case and substitutes this one in its place before we can arrive on the scene."

Holmes steepled together his long, thin fingers.

"I can assure you, gentlemen, there is only one jewel case in this affair, and this is that case."

"Impossible," said Lestrade. "We know he couldn't have removed the jewels from the case before throwing it from the train, and there wasn't time enough for him, or his accomplice, to pick the lock, remove the jewels, and substitute his playing card unobserved, before Symmonds climbed down the embankment."

Holmes sat forward suddenly. "The train has started."

"The constables at Lewes are waiting for us. We can conduct a full search of all the passengers on the train at the station," Lestrade said.

Holmes laughed, "Of course!"

Lestrade was stung. "You have your clever ways of knowing things, Mr. Holmes, but sometimes it comes down to manpower in cases like these." The train had rolled forward and come to rest in the station with a hiss of steam and scream of the brakes. Lestrade rose to his feet.

"The jewels never left London," Holmes said.

"You mean this is all a hoax?" Lestrade demanded. "An insurance scam?"

"No, the robbery is genuine, but it occurred before Lady Kildaire ever boarded the train. This whole case-snatching was just for show, to make it appear the robbery had only just occurred."

"But why draw attention to it at all?" I asked. "Why not simply take the jewels and no one the wiser?"

"Someone is always bound to notice when a set of valuables goes missing. But *when* it was taken has a way of obscuring *who* took it."

"Is that so?" Lestrade said. "I don't suppose you have any further information you'd like to share that would put us on the track of this Jack of Diamonds character?"

"As to that," said Holmes, "I expect he is long gone. Most likely he left the train as soon as we pulled into Lewes, possibly disguised as a signalman or a constable. You'll have better luck arresting his accomplice."

"His accomplice?" Lestrade objected. "You said his throwing the case from the train was nothing but a false scent to take us off his trail!"

"Unless I am mistaken, you will find Lady Kildaire's maid most willing to assist you in your investigation after she discovers she has lost both her lover and the fortune in jewels he promised her. Poor girl. Still, it's not a hanging offense, is it?"

Made in the USA
Lexington, KY
06 September 2018